PRAISE F

THE LOUDNESS OF

'My heart grew, then broke, then mended itself. A wise, funny, brave novel and a story that you will never want to forget.'

FAVEL PARRETT

'so cleverly structured and full of little golden nuggets of text that just take your breath away. It manages to cover so many themes, including trauma, mental health, family relationships and grief, yet still give depth to each one ... *The Loudness of Unsaid Things* will be one of my most recommended books of this year.'

READINGS MONTHLY

'Susie is a little girl lost. It's hard not to feel your heart break as loneliness, confusion and so many unsaid things dog a child-hood unfairly complicated by adult problems and tragedy. This impressive debut novel by Hilde Hinton ... has been rightly compared to the acclaimed *Boy Swallows Universe* and *Eleanor Oliphant is Completely Fine*.'

HERALD SUN

'insightful and emotionally gripping ... Hinton has in Susie captured the complexities of a child becoming an adult too fast, one whose independence is as alienating to her peers as it is captivating.'

SYDNEY MORNING HERALD

'Hilde Hinton's debut novel is character-driven storytelling at its best ... Hinton's style is direct, conversational, and often funny, despite the subject matter ... Hinton has an ear for dialogue and an eye for detail, but her work's greatest asset is its heart. Her moving, well-realised debut introduces a promising Australian writer.'

AUSTRALIAN BOOK REVIEW

'a heartbreaking, ultimately hopeful book ... It's sad, but also wry and irreverent.'

THE AUSTRALIAN WOMEN'S WEEKLY

'This stunning debut novel is about family, loneliness and isolation ... Your heart will grow, then break and then mend itself again as you follow the story of Miss Kaye, who works at The Institute, a place for the damaged, and Susie, a young girl who reflects on the things she wanted to say but never could.'

MARIE CLAIRE

'Hinton's writing style is colloquial and engaging, familiar and inviting. Reading *The Loudness of Unsaid Things* is like listening to the tales of a friend with a fascinating life story and a special knack for storytelling ... This is a quintessentially Australian coming-of-age tale, with wonderfully complex, funny and heart-breaking female characters.'

OSCAR AND FRIENDS

A SOLITARY WALK ON THE MOON

ALSO BY HILDE HINTON

The Loudness of Unsaid Things
Heroes Next Door

A SOLITARY WALK ON THE MOON

Hilde Hinton

Published in Australia and New Zealand in 2022
by Hachette Australia
(an imprint of Hachette Australia Pty Limited)
Gadigal Country, Level 17, 207 Kent Street, Sydney, NSW 2000
www.hachette.com.au

Hachette Australia acknowledges and pays our respects to the past, present and
future Traditional Owners and Custodians of Country throughout Australia
and recognises the continuation of cultural, spiritual and educational practices
of Aboriginal and Torres Strait Islander peoples. Our head office is located on
the lands of the Gadigal people of the Eora Nation.

 A catalogue record for this
book is available from the
National Library of Australia

ISBN: 978 0 7336 4704 8 (paperback)

Cover design by Christabella Designs
Cover artwork courtesy of Elizabeth Mayville
Author photograph courtesy of Dez Stallard
Typeset in 12/19.5 pt Sabon LT Pro by Bookhouse
Printed and bound in Australia by McPherson's Printing Group

 The paper this book is printed on is certified against the
Forest Stewardship Council® Standards. McPherson's Printing
Group holds FSC® chain of custody certification SA-COC-005379.
FSC® promotes environmentally responsible, socially beneficial
and economically viable management of the world's forests.

PROLOGUE

The man tied the haphazard bunch of flowers he had picked from overgrown gardens between the old house and the cemetery with a burgundy hair tie he had bribed from his daughter's wrist. The eight-year-old girl tended towards quiet, but today she had been silent; and had stared attentively at him more often, and for longer, than usual. It made sense. He hadn't tried to coax her to the surface, nor instigated any conversation at all. Not today. Today he could barely coax himself.

His father who wasn't his father had died a year ago exactly, and he had returned to clear out the house that had been overrun by time. The past, the verve, the memories had dissipated. The remaining furniture, hanging clothes and dishes seemed so brittle that he wondered if they would disintegrate in his hands on the way to the big blue battered skip bin.

He placed the awkward posy on the headstone and looked over at his daughter, who had sat on a nearby grave to wait for him. She politely feigned interest in her surroundings, and he appreciated that she wouldn't see his welling eyes, his shaky legs, his wobbly innards. After trying to steady himself on the stone balls across the top of the epitaph, he let himself fall to his knees. Then he crawled across the top of the slab, lay on his back and placed his hands across his chest as though the gesture would keep him in place.

The brink of sleep was alluring, but he resisted, stood up and shook himself back together.

'Fish and chips?' he asked his daughter, who jumped up and took his hand.

They ate on the old bench in his childhood park before setting off to the house that had been sucked dry by time.

PART ONE

CHAPTER ONE

*E*velyn stood and stared at the colour swatches in the paint store. It wasn't her first time. Last time she had to navigate all the whites. Laundromats are traditionally white, but now she felt that hers was a little too sterile, and she wanted to paint one wall blue. It was important to maintain tradition as well as provide a fresh and bright environment for the customers waiting for their wash cycles to finish. To boost the atmosphere, she also had some board games and books in her office to lend out. Each game had a list of contained pieces, which she dutifully checked when each game was returned. The Monopoly was, however, missing a Fleet Street, and she had done her best to recreate one with some textas and the back of an unwanted birthday card.

Her previous experience at the paint shop, with the myriad of white paint options, had not prepared her at all for this sea of blues. She felt just as overwhelmed as last time.

'Can I help you?' a dishevelled man asked her. She wondered why he hadn't at least trimmed what was trying to be a beard on his chin.

'I want blue. The colour a fire engine would be if fire engines were blue,' she said without taking her eyes off the blue cards. She was sure it would have jumped out of the display if it had existed. What particularly upset her were the names versus the colours. 'Hello Sailor' sounded sassy, but was too dark and flat for its name. 'Garter Blue' had no vibrancy and was more midnight. 'Boudoir Blue' was devoid of love, 'Daring Indigo' was virtually black and 'Tropical Bird' bore no resemblance to any feather she had ever seen. Even in the bird park in Kuala Lumpur. As she reeled off these discrepancies to the untidy man, she thought he might have smiled under his moustache, but she was too absorbed in the blues to know for sure. Which was lucky for him because she certainly did not have a sense of humour that morning.

'And what, may I ask, does "Flemish Blue" mean?' she asked as she flicked the card with her finger numerous times. 'Last time I checked, Dutchmen weren't blue at all.' Her outrage was taking the wind out of her sails, and she felt immediately weary. The untidy man noticed her deflation and suggested that a half-strength 'Hello Sailor' may well be the blue a fire engine would be if fire engines were blue. Evelyn picked it up, tried to imagine it at half strength and put the card back despondently.

'How about I mix you a sample pot,' he said with kindness. 'It's only six dollars and I believe it's worth the risk.'

Evelyn ummed and ahhed, looked him up and down and concluded that he may well have the knowledge to produce what she was after – even if his shorts were too short. But not before a reference check. His name was Don and he had been selling paint since he was a teenager. He waxed lyrical about paint stores of the past versus the in-and-out nature of the modern store.

'Back then, we used to *talk* with people. Ask what they were doing and picture their lives in the colours,' he said wistfully.

'Well, I need a bit of colour in my laundromat. Blue is calming and I want people to relax while they wait,' she said. 'It's all too white at the moment.'

He asked about the layout of her laundromat, and she explained that she wanted the wall that faced people as they walked in to be blue. The wall that had the stable-style door to her office where she stored the immaculately folded full-service washing upon completion. He asked what white was on the walls currently. She flicked the back of her hand at the plethora of whites and said she didn't have the strength to discuss it.

'Navigating that was just too much,' she said. He smiled and ushered her over to the counter. Propping herself on her elbows, she watched him type some numbers into the screen. Then they watched three colours pour into the sample pot and stop with precision. He gently hammered the lid on with a rubber mallet and placed it on the mixing machine. The small can was shaken to within an inch of its life.

'It would make an interesting carnival ride,' Don said as he moved towards her. They watched until it was finished. It was no carnival ride Evelyn would venture on. Her limits were the merry-go-round and the Ferris wheel. Why someone would pay money to be tossed and turned and spun about was beyond her. Besides, life was equally tumultuous – and it was free.

Don took the can out, placed it on the counter with a flourish and edged his mini screwdriver around its lid before popping it off and revealing a rich grey blue. Like a river on a sunny day, but towards dusk as it was a little faded.

'It's a most lovely blue,' she said as she shook her head. 'But it is *not* the colour of a fire engine if fire engines were blue.'

'Well,' Don said confidently, 'I think that is exactly the colour of a fire engine if fire engines were blue. It's majestic.'

They stared into the can together for a few moments.

'I'll take four litres, thanks,' she said, standing up straight, 'even if it is *not* the right colour.' On occasion she lost her grace, and she was pleased that she hadn't lost her cool this time, despite the lack of brightness in her paint. He was right; it was majestic, and perhaps more calming than the blue in her head. Don seemed to debate whether to say something more and wisely decided that it was time for him to be quiet. He mixed the full can and they silently watched the whole process with equal interest again. He rang up the sale and Evelyn turned to leave.

'Thank you,' she said over her shoulder. It almost hurt.

'If you need a hand painting the wall, let me know,' he said. 'I have Sundays and Mondays off and I'm happy to help.'

Evelyn was a perfectly capable woman who could paint a wall by herself, thank you very much, and she was in no mood to accept assistance. She did, however, take the piece of paper on which he had written his number and place it in her pocket. With a brief, sharp nod, she left the store and headed back to the laundromat. She needed to be manning the desk for the full-service wash drop-offs by eight thirty sharp, so people could get about their busy days. Also, it was Tuesday, and the skinny, spotty mother who clearly found the world too difficult always brought in her little boy, who asked 'Why?' more than most, on Tuesday afternoons. Evelyn had the answers to last week's three questions ready and looked forward to satisfying some of his many curiosities.

CHAPTER TWO

*E*velyn had ten minutes to spare by the time she got back to the laundromat. Rather than make a coffee, she opened the top half of her stable-style door, placed the round silver bell on the lower door's inbuilt ledge, neatened her clothing, ran her hands through her thick, wiry hair and tied it up in a loose bun. Her hair was still mostly rich chocolate brown with one in a hundred or so being a dirty grey. She always said she would never dye her hair and looked forward to having a full head of white hair, but she had been dealt a dirty grey. After much internal debate, she decided that was the way it was and if she was allotted dirty grey, then dirty grey it would be. For a while she washed her hair more often, but it made no difference to the dirty grey, so she had begun using it as a camouflage and an excuse to wash her hair less.

She lived above the laundromat, and the bathroom still had a matching lime green basin and bath from the 1950s. The showerhead above the bath was fixed, but it wasn't so high that she was forced to wet her hair each time. She wondered if it was set lower because people were shorter back then. Evelyn enjoyed having the world at her fingertips and had gone online to discover she would have been five foot three in 1958, rather than her current five foot seven. On further inspection, she would have been five foot one at the start of World War I. So, she knocked the mystery of the showerhead height off her list and concluded that she had been correct. When they installed the showerhead in the 1950s, it would have wet her hair every shower.

The morning passed as all the mornings did. She ticketed the full-service wash drop-offs and began washing, drying and folding the loads, making sure all the while that there were available machines for any walk-ins. Once, and only once, Evelyn had taken up too many machines on a day when walk-ins came in higher numbers than usual. On that day, the clients were moaning to each other about the machine hog who had taken up the other machines as they pointed at Evelyn's full-service washing loads and rolled their eyes. Evelyn had paced around her small office storage area feeling guilty and pretended she had no idea whose loads they belonged to. That way they wouldn't know it was her.

She had tried so hard not to intervene in their debates about who was next for the dryers. Laundromat etiquette was a complex business. Do you get priority if you wait for your washing? What if there is a wet load waiting in a basket near the dryer, but the person isn't there to put the clothes in – does the next person get right of way? What if your load finishes first but you go for a walk and the vigilant person who stays and waits for their washing puts their load in the dryer twenty seconds before you arrive back? What if a person decides to split their load between two dryers, while a growing bank of washing sits there getting more and more dank by the second?

On the day Evelyn had tried very hard not to intervene, she had intervened. It did not help. By the time she walked out into the main room, waggling her finger and trying to change the world order, she had worked herself up into quite a frenzy. She was talking through gritted teeth and mumbling away to the point that the recipients of her ramblings assumed her to be mentally unwell. At least Evelyn had the presence of mind to realise she was not actually helping, and closed her office, put a 'Back in one hour' sign on the stable-style door and went out for a long walk. Most of that walk was spent worrying about the fact that anyone needing her services would, in fact, have no idea when this hour started or finished, and she chastised herself for not leaving a sign that stipulated a return time. This realisation hit her so hard she slapped her forehead over and over, but her distress couldn't be tamed. By the time she had returned, the walk-ins had finished their cycles and she was able to move her loads into the dryers. She vowed never to intervene in laundromat etiquette issues again.

On this particular Tuesday, Evelyn made her way through the full-service washes without hogging the machines. A few self-serve customers came in and out and responded pleasantly to Evelyn's welcoming smiles. At two o'clock, she put up the 'Back in five minutes' sign (this did not need a return time) and raced over to the bakery. This was the time they reduced the prices on the items they knew would go to waste before close. As Evelyn perused the sale items, she thought of young Ben who would be in with his mother after school.

The first time she had offered him a snack, she had asked his mother about potential allergies and acted casually, so his mother would not think Evelyn had gone out of her way to get snacks. She presented them as leftovers, and muttered a comment about how much food goes to waste these days. Ben's mother had been nonchalant and seemed relieved that Evelyn was distracting her son from directing his endless questions and chatter towards her. The boy could talk, that's for sure, but Evelyn didn't mind.

Today, Evelyn chose some mini quiches and a matchstick pastry for Ben and party pies and a custard tart for herself. While Cheryl, the baker's wife, bundled up her order they had a chat about the upcoming council meeting. A developer was trying to build a block of ten units at the end of the street. The metal and glass structure was going to reduce the charm of the old, well preserved inner city suburb, and both Evelyn and Cheryl were keen to watch its potential impact on the parking spots along the shopping strip. A year or so ago, the council had brought in two-hour parking on the street, which most of the shopkeepers were pleased with. It stopped traders like Bruno the shoe man from parking outside their stores all day. He always took up parks outside other people's shops, so he wasn't blocking customers from parking outside his store. Cheryl and Evelyn had spent many an hour tut-tutting about this. Evelyn had told Cheryl that if she had a car, she would park it outside Bruno's store to see how he liked it. Cheryl said she did have a car, and began parking outside Bruno's store to demonstrate how frustrating it was. For a while, there had been a few shouting matches between the shopkeepers as everyone began parking outside each other's stores.

Evelyn was grateful when the council brought in two-hour parking and all the store holders found alternative parking in neighbouring streets, and then pretended there had never been any discord in the first place – which pleased Evelyn no end. The reunification had been seamless and they all returned to blaming the council for their woes instead of each other.

When Evelyn returned to the laundromat, she took Mr Keenan's business shirts out of the dryer and set up her ironing board. The ironing component of her offered services was quite lucrative. There were fandangled steamers and whatnot available for purchase quite cheaply at appliance stores, and Evelyn had dutifully investigated them. But she decided in the end that nothing beat her good old iron, so she did things the old-fashioned way. She took great care and pride in her ironing. Mr Keenan's requirement was, however, rather unusual. He liked his collared shirts ironed with creases, so it looked like they had just come out of the packet. He had told her he wanted his clients to think he wore a new shirt every day. Evelyn had refrained from saying that most people washed and ironed their clothes before wear, but each to their own. Perhaps if she hadn't been so excited by this new challenge, she would have put him right back in his box on the matter.

The first time she ironed his shirts, she had spent an exorbitant amount on a man's shirt at Myer so she could unfold it from its packet and iron the creases in most exactly. She had used the cardboard from the packet that held the shirt in place, traced it on some specially bought card and made ten exact replicas so she could present Mr Keenan with pretend bought shirts in a professional manner. Mr Keenan had nodded approvingly the first time he collected his shirts and promised to bring in the cardboard inserts each time he dropped off the washing. Evelyn knew she had a lifetime customer by the way he smiled at her initial presentation. Mr Keenan also had an eye for detail and picked up his shirts at the same time and day each week, and always paid with the correct money. Evelyn had an EFTPOS machine, but Mr Keenan always paid his thirty-six dollars with a twenty, a ten, a five and a one-dollar coin. Evelyn always had his receipt ready so as not to hold him up.

Evelyn hummed away as she ironed his shirts with precision and was only returned to the world when young Ben ran into the store calling her name.

'Evie, Evie,' he called out as he dropped his schoolbag outside her stable-style door and poked his head over the ledge.

'Hello, young man,' Evie said as she turned the iron off. She walked over and ruffled his curly blond hair. It was getting so long at the front that she could barely see his big hazel eyes. Ben darted his eyes around the office and rested them on the white paper bags on her desk containing the bakery delights. Evelyn asked if he had room in his tummy for some food. He nodded vigorously and said 'Yes, please.' She congratulated him on his manners and, as she placed his mini quiches in the microwave, she asked him about his day. As is the way with children, he said 'Good, thanks.' Rather than tell him this answer was unsatisfactory, because never does a day go by without something of interest happening, she asked him whether anything funny had occurred.

Ben rattled off a tale about how Sam from grade two, who was really big for his age, had come around a corner and run full pelt into little Hannah from prep.

'There was blood everywhere,' Ben said in a serious tone. 'But it was also kind of funny,' he added momentarily.

Evelyn said it was important not to laugh at other people's misfortunes, and Ben said he wasn't laughing at that, but at the miniscule chance of this collision even happening. Evelyn smiled as she placed the mini quiches on a bread plate and handed it to him.

In the meantime, Ben's mother had arrived and placed her load into a machine. As always, she ignored Evelyn completely, sat on a chair and pulled out her mobile phone. Evelyn didn't mind. She came out and sat at the green formica table in the middle of the laundromat with Ben. In between mouthfuls, he said that the school called an emergency assembly and told everyone that they had to be careful and thoughtful of others. Evelyn and Ben debated whether it was more important to be careful or let yourself lose an intense game of tiggy.

'They're going to paint snails on the dangerous corners and kids have to slow down when they see the snails,' Ben said. Evelyn thought this was a good idea and said so, but then asked Ben why they wouldn't just write 'slow down' in words.

'The prep kids can't read yet,' Ben said, and Evelyn nodded in approval.

When he'd polished off his quiches, his eyes wandered over to the stable-style door.

'Is there any room in your tummy for cake?' Evelyn asked.

'Der,' Ben said as he nodded vigorously.

Rather than point out alternative communication strategies, Evelyn smiled and went to get his matchstick. She thought she saw tears in his eyes when he opened the bag, but it was so fleeting that she couldn't be sure. Evelyn suddenly remembered that she had picked up a two-litre chocolate-flavoured milk from the supermarket the previous evening. Its use-by date was today, so it had been half price. Ben was thrilled and gulped down a large glass in one go. Not for the first time, Evelyn wondered whether his mother fed him properly. The woman was stick thin and Evelyn worried whether she could even look after herself, let alone Ben.

Evelyn took her notebook from her apron pocket and Ben settled his backside into his chair.

'Do you remember last week's questions?' she asked, knowing that he did. She asked which one he wanted answered first.

'Why do ships float?' he asked. Evelyn began a drawn-out explanation of displacement. Ben looked like she was talking Flemish. 'Come on, young man,' she said, ushering him through to her office. Past the main room there was a lean-to off the back of the building. There was a laundry sink out there. She picked up a bucket and they watched the sink fill together. It wasn't the beach, but the sound of running water soothed them both. When the sink was nearly full, Evelyn asked him to push the empty bucket down into the water.

'It's hard to push down, Evie,' he said, surprised.

'That's displacement!' Evelyn said proudly. 'The water has to move to allow for the bucket, but it's not happy, is it?' Ben said he understood now and asked about how planes stay in the air as they walked back out the front. Evelyn explained how the shape of the wings caused air pressure, and that air wanted to be with itself, and how it pushed up with all its might to reunite with the air above the wings, thereby holding up the aeroplane. Ben was impressed by this, but Evelyn could see some doubt in his eyes. She rushed through to the last question, as she didn't quite understand air pressure herself. She had a new understanding of the difficulty of being a teacher since meeting Ben. Lastly, she told him there were seven hundred types of dinosaurs but there may well be more to be discovered. He asked her to name all seven hundred. She said she could barely list three, and that finding out would take until he was nine.

By this stage Ben's mother had thrown her washing into a striped bag and was urging Ben to hurry up. Ben protested and said that he hadn't had time to present Evelyn with next week's three questions, but his mum did not care. Evelyn raced to the back and grabbed the party pies and custard tart she had bought for herself. She said she didn't want to see them going to waste, even though her tummy was rumbling, and Ben's mum muttered a thanks as she snatched the paper bag, put it in the washing bag and took Ben's arm rather too firmly.

'See you next week, Ben,' Evelyn called after him. He didn't turn around but he threw his free arm over his shoulder in a wave. Evelyn shook her head briskly and walked back inside to wait for the full-service wash pickups.

CHAPTER THREE

*E*velyn woke early the next morning. The sun wasn't up, and the birds weren't chirping yet. She tried lying there in the hope of falling back to sleep. Then she turned on the radio so the background noise would deter her brain from running too fast. She chose a classical music station and let herself fall into the music. As she imagined herself playing lead violin, she fell into a stressful half sleep that had her chasing a non-existent blue like her life depended on it. When the news theme music came on, it woke her rather than threading its way into the dream. Although she was tired, she was relieved to be out of the chase. She checked the weather on her phone before dressing in the appropriate number of layers.

It was the annoying time of year where it was layers on and off all day. She put her fleecy lined vest on over a light jumper for a morning stroll, then put on her sturdy boots and set off towards the local park. There were always a few dog walkers who preferred to get the walk out of the way before work. There was a labradoodle named Nutmeg that was often out and about with his owner at this time of day. He was still a puppy and growing fast before Evelyn's eyes. The young man who walked him had kind eyes, but trained the puppy with steely consistency. Evelyn thought it said a great deal about the man himself and she thought he would be a wonderful father.

Down near the station there was a coffee cart that opened at five, and today Evelyn only had to wait a few minutes before it opened. It was operated by a tired looking middle-aged couple who hadn't realised the toll of small business when they'd bought into the franchise. At first, they had been so welcoming and big-eyed, now they were just bleary-eyed and bordering on robotic. Regardless of her state of mind, Evelyn always pushed weariness down to the bottom of her boots rather than let a customer see her insides. Instead of lecturing the couple on professionalism, she ordered a long black with a dash of cold water please and half turned to look down the street, rather than enter forced unwelcome conversation. After receiving her coffee, she headed to the park and sat on a bench. Her bench.

She looked around for Nutmeg, but there were no puppies to be found. There was, however, the old man who drifted into the laundromat irregularly. He was wearing his trademark beige suit and red handkerchief in the breast pocket.

Since opening the laundromat, Evelyn had noticed he was becoming more and more forgetful. His face had changed from confident and content to confused, and he rarely brushed or cut his hair anymore. Or washed his clothes as regularly. When she had picked up on his deterioration some time back, she had followed him home one evening. For his safety, of course. She tailed him using the strategies she had learnt many years ago from Enid Blyton mystery books. Stay a certain distance away, pop in and out of available shadows at differing intervals, pretend to look in shop windows and such. She had followed him to a 1960s cream brick apartment building but remained unaware of which unit was his.

As the sun peeked up, a ray caught the star on his belt buckle and Evelyn smiled as it twinkled briefly into the atmosphere. It was an oversized buckle that belonged on a cowboy from an old movie, and he was obviously attached to it. Each time she had seen him around the neighbourhood he had been wearing it. In the growing light, she noticed he wasn't carrying his drink bottle. He always carried a glass drink bottle with a push-in metal top with a metal ring as a handle. The bottle swung alongside him as he walked. When he took a sip, he always sat on a bench, removed its top and basked in slow mouthfuls. As if it was the only water he had access to for weeks. Once, as he savoured each sip, she wondered if it was grappa, moonshine or bootleg. The way he drank indicated a quiet dignity, and Evelyn wondered what he used to be.

Today the old man walked one way for a few steps, then the other, then south, then north. He seemed to have no idea where he was going. His face looked like he had walked into a room and then wondered why he had entered it in the first place. Evelyn was familiar with this feeling, but couldn't imagine what it must be like to experience it all the time. She got up and headed over to the man slowly, so she wouldn't startle him. As she moved closer, an idea came to her.

'Hello,' she said cheerfully as though they were old friends. He looked at her, clearly wondering whether he was supposed to know her. 'You live in the same building as me,' she said. 'Should we walk back together? It's a little frightening being a lady on her own at this hour.' She believed men liked to be needed – especially forgetful ones. It seemed to work, and he walked alongside her. She stayed one step out to the left and half a step behind. Evelyn thought this was a superb way to get him home with his integrity intact and she babbled on and on about the laundromat as she walked. Small stuff, like her upcoming blue wall, the rise of electricity charges, the monstrosity they were planning to build at the end of the main street. He let her talk. When they got to the cream brick apartment building, Evelyn patted herself down for keys. While she was doing that, she saw recognition in his eyes, and he pushed his hand deep down into his front left pocket and pulled out a key. He used it to open the outer door and she thanked him when he held it open for her.

Evelyn walked straight ahead, and the man peeled off down the left-hand corridor to his apartment. She doubled back and peeked around the corner. He went inside number three, and she memorised it in case she needed to be helpful again. Then she slipped back out the front door and strode jauntily back to the laundromat.

She wanted to check her painting supplies to make sure she had enough good brushes, enough light sandpaper and a usable roller. Nothing worse than starting a job without the correct equipment. After a cup of coffee, she put on her apron and opened her booth.

The day went slowly. Nothing out of the ordinary, no interesting characters, although she spent forty-five minutes glaring at a shoeless man with dreadlocks who came in. He seemed oblivious to Evelyn's feelings and spoke very loudly on his phone. He made call after call looking for a couch to sleep on and eventually hit paydirt as he pulled all his bedding from the dryer and put it in a large blue, red and white striped plastic bag. Without folding it. While he sat there, he sprawled over three chairs and even had his feet on the seats. Evelyn was convinced he had put other customers off entering. When he walked out, she spray-and-wiped the padded vinyl chairs and placed them back neatly against the wall.

She'd shrugged him off by the time the day ended, and returned to the hardware store. Her roller was clumpy, and even though they often came back to life in the paint tray, she thought this one needed to retire. Other than that, she was prepared for her blue wall.

At the hardware store, she headed straight to the paint section. There were a variety of rollers, but she always preferred the barely there ones. No thick fur, a short-haired roller. Synthetic, for even spread.

'I'm available Sunday to help with that wall,' Don said from behind her.

It gave her such a fright she dropped her roller. Don retrieved it and handed it to her. After she explained that it was impolite to come up behind people and frighten them, to which he nodded with a ridiculous almost smile around the corner of his mouth, he actually apologised. Evelyn was not impressed but found herself almost smiling as well. It was important to stick to one's guns, so she didn't let the issue escape. He could cause a heart attack going around scaring people like that. Don proceeded to say that it was difficult to get an even coat with a bold colour.

'I'm aware of that,' she said in a clipped tone that seemed to go unnoticed.

He launched into a three-coat method, vertical first, horizontal second, then back to vertical. Then he added that the rolls needed to be staggered to avoid subtle lines. By this stage she had forgotten how annoyed she was and supposed that perhaps she ought to consider his offer of help after all.

'I need to think about it,' she said as she put her hands up, palms out. There was no room for any more information in her throbbing head. Before taking her leave, she said she'd call him the day before if she needed him.

Evelyn went around the corner of the store to wait and see what kind of car Don got into after he finished work. Waiting had never been an issue for Evelyn. There were people to look at, so she entertained herself with the passers-by. After a time, Don came out and walked straight through the carpark. Like herself he obviously lived within walking distance of the store. It briefly crossed her mind that she shouldn't be following him but this way, if he ever disappeared, she would at least be able to check his residence. People died at home all the time and sometimes they weren't discovered for weeks. Although he grated on her nerves, she would hate that to happen to him.

Don had no idea she was ducking in and out of trees and doorways only twenty metres behind him. When he entered a bottle shop in a small, tired strip of shops, Evelyn walked into a nearby medical centre to avoid detection. She made small talk with the receptionist, asked about fee gaps, whether they did the Medicare rebate on the spot and eventually left the medical centre with three different doctors' business cards. The receptionist had been most patient with her enquiries, and Evelyn thanked her.

By the time she emerged, there was no sign of Don. She looked up and down the street, and headed to the next intersection. He wasn't up or down that street either. She chastised herself for taking too long at the medical centre and headed back to the bottle shop herself. She liked a wine from time to time and thought it would be good to have some around the place, especially in case Don would like a glass should she call to ask for his assistance. After perusing the shelves, she decided on a chardonnay (her favourite), a merlot (in case it was Don's favourite) and a bottle of champagne (in case a celebratory blue wall drink should be in order). She contemplated buying some red ribbon to place in front of the wall for its official opening, but she didn't want Don to think her odd, so she walked straight past the newsagency and headed home.

CHAPTER FOUR

*F*or the rest of the week, Evelyn didn't see anyone who needed to be followed home in case of emergencies, although there was one couple that came close. The whole time they sat in the laundromat, through both wash and dry cycles, the man paced around gesticulating wildly. He certainly had a bee in his bonnet. He was almost on his knees when he implored the woman that they stick together because the people who worked for them were dickheads, and she had to support him and not pay them so much heed.

Evelyn was finding it all a little difficult to follow, but there had obviously been a dispute with their neighbour when a staff member had taken out the rubbish bin.

'He shouldn't have whinged about the fucking bin if he didn't want me to do something about it,' the man said in a crescendo as he walked in circles. His companion tried to explain that he had misinterpreted the whole affair because the neighbour was actually offering spare bin space if they needed it, and there was no dispute in the first place. But the man wasn't listening. In the end the woman told him he was right (he wasn't) and that she was there to support him (she shouldn't be wasting her time). The washing was nearly finished by the time he finally fell onto one of the vinyl chairs, fully spent from expressing all his feelings.

He was still muttering about how they had to be united, be a team, because no other fucker mattered – they weren't important (except for him). Evelyn noted that each time he had seen her staring, he toned down his tirades a little.

'I need a coffee,' he said, and left the laundromat.

'Are you okay?' Evelyn asked the woman in her most welcoming tone.

The woman said she was fine and rolled her eyes before moving the washing to the dryer. She explained that he was a sensitive man who had trouble dealing with his feelings, and that everything was A-okay. Then she introduced herself and said they had just opened a tattoo studio down the way. Evelyn had noticed the new store, which had replaced a bead shop.

She was sad for the lady who had been so passionate about beads. One day, Evelyn had spent some time looking down the aisles of containers, each brimming with a different bead. One bucket had been full of mini ice-cream cones, and she had bought them to make into earrings, even though her ears weren't pierced. Somewhere along the line they were sure to come in handy. But at fifty cents a pop, she had a feeling the shop wouldn't last too long. And the bead lady had a disappointing lack of interest in the local people. Perhaps she was shy, but, in Evelyn's view, refusing to engage with customers did not make for good business. The pair of mini ice-cream cones were still sitting in Evelyn's 'you never know' drawer.

When the passive aggressive full-of-feelings man came back to the laundromat (with one coffee), the lady, who had introduced herself as Ash, called Evelyn over and introduced her to Matt. He became a little sheepish and said he was sorry for carrying on in her laundromat, and added it was nice to meet a good neighbour. He even did air quotation marks on 'good'. Evelyn did not like air quotation marks, but she was chuffed that she was considered a good neighbour. Because she was.

'Better get back to it,' Evelyn said as she gave Ash a supportive shoulder squeeze. When they left the shop with their washing (folded by Ash alone), Evelyn placed the couple at the top of her watch list.

That evening, Evelyn got out Don's number and sat at her jigsaw table upstairs. She contemplated what to say should Don answer and what message to leave should Don not answer. Evelyn did not like answering machines, despite appreciating their practicality. She was working on a jigsaw of old book bindings on thick wooden shelves and completed four face-out titles before she had the courage to call. When she picked up the phone, she put it straight back down. A glass of wine was in order, as a glass or two always made her appear more friendly. After downing two wines in quick succession, she dialled the number. It rang a few times before going to voicemail. She listened to Don say that she'd called Don and to please leave a message.

'Hello, Don, this is Evelyn. Blue paint,' she managed to say. 'Anyway, if the offer to assist me with my wall still stands, please call me back on the number that came up on your screen.' Evelyn hung up the phone and got a fit of the giggles. She drank her next glass of wine more slowly and managed a whole shelf of her jigsaw before going to bed.

CHAPTER FIVE

*A*fter an awkward phone call where Evelyn managed to both ask for help with her wall and set a time for Sunday evening, it was arranged. Evelyn had suggested that she would tape around the wall to prevent bleeding, but Don said it was best to get it on as close to painting time as possible, and to get it off as soon as the cutting in was complete. At five o'clock she closed the store and put up a sign in the window saying 'Closed for renovation, reopen at eight thirty am Monday'. This way she wouldn't miss her regulars. It was important to grasp onto them, as new habits form quickly and she didn't want her customers to go elsewhere.

She carefully pulled out her drop sheets, tray, brushes, her new roller and a bag of rags. These were largely made up of forgotten or abandoned clothing in her machines that didn't make the op shop grade. She loved dropping things at her local op shop as she felt like she was contributing. It also gave her a reason to scan the usually tattered and outdated books in the hope that, just once, she would find something desirable that she hadn't read. Evelyn was reluctant to try new authors at new prices, so she experimented with the op shop books. Even then she sat in the shop to read the first twenty pages before making a commitment. She also picked up the odd jigsaw. Only one had ever contained all the pieces, plus two bonus pieces from another. She tutted and wondered why it was so difficult to donate usable items. She donated the jigsaws back but had the decency to tape a note to them saying how many pieces were missing.

Evelyn was just putting out some cheeses and biccies on the formica table when there was a sharp knock on the window. Startled, she looked up to see Don grinning through the glass. At least he had the decency not to lean on the glass and smear it. She managed a smile and a brisk wave as she headed over to let him in. He handed her a bottle of champagne and said perhaps they could christen the new wall upon completion. Evelyn laughed, despite not wanting to, and told him how she had been to the newsagency on Wattle Grove and nearly bought a red ribbon to cut and officially open the blue wall, but decided against it in case he thought her odd. He guffawed and asked why she would be at that strip of shops when there was a perfectly good one up the road. Evelyn's face went pink as she remembered she had been following Don, and she covered it by saying there was a customer who was terribly forgetful near Wattle Grove. She had been there to drop in on him, to see that he hadn't left the stove on and had eaten some food.

'I must do some research on Alzheimer's and dementia,' she added, pulling her notebook out of her apron pocket to add this task to her to-do list.

'You're a good person, Evelyn,' Don said. He appeared genuine, and Evelyn flushed again. She held up a decanter of red wine and an empty glass and Don nodded in approval. They had a brief discussion about red wine being called claret back in the day, with no conclusion as to what it was called now, as Don began laying the drop sheet with precision. Evelyn had two rolls of masking tape, and they chatted about things that had changed names over the years. Manic depression had become bipolar, and they agreed that manic depression was much more accurate; and Don hadn't been aware that aprons had originally been called naprons.

By the time they exhausted their list of changed names and agreed that their filing cabinet brains were so full these days it was hard to access anything at all, the wall was taped. Evelyn stood back and admired their work. She talked of the benefits of planning when taking on any task and Don wholeheartedly agreed. She was going to suggest that he plan to trim his beard to look more respectable, but she bit her tongue. Without talking, they both sat at the same time to have some more wine and nibble on some biccies. He complimented her on her range of biscuits, as not everyone likes wafer thin crackers or mini toast squares. He kept eating the sea salt crackers that Evelyn found a little soft.

'I'm more Jatz than Clix,' she said, pre-deciding he was clearly Clix. He was.

Don got out his key ring and used a specific paint can opener to open the blue paint. She handed him a yellow plastic stirrer that had triangles cut into it. Evelyn figured those holes were good for mixing, so the paint had more swirl room. He slapped it on his hand a few times and then explained he was an old-fashioned painter and asked whether there might be some wayward sticks out the back.

'Well, there's a tree,' she said, as she stood up.

'Where there's a tree, there are sticks,' Don said as he stood too. Evelyn felt most put out. She had not intended on Don walking through her space at all. She quickly surmised that he may need the toilet at some stage and pushed her angst to the bottom of her work shoes. She led the way through the stable door, her ironing room, the back kitchenette, past the laundry/toilet outbuilding to a small rectangle of cracked concrete with a tree in the middle.

'Oh, a Japanese maple,' Don said as he softly caressed some leaves. Evelyn was surprised by his gentle reaction and let him be for the smallest of moments. However, there were no sticks. When Evelyn suggested they choose a small branch to break off, Don pointed out that dead sticks were best.

'We'll just have to go on an excursion,' he said with his hands palms up and a smile in his eyes. This was an unexpected development. Usually Evelyn didn't like unexpected developments but, whether it was the wine or an unusual acceptance of plan deviation, she found herself nodding and leading the way back to the front. Don closed the paint can and stomped on the lid gently. He dusted off his dustless hands and put out a crooked elbow. Then he bowed and asked Madame if she was ready for their Sunday walk. Evelyn put her forearm in his and off they went out the front door.

Don had set the scene and Evelyn joined in wholeheartedly. They commented on the imaginary olden-day town before them as they walked down the street. Evelyn admired the new manor house being built on the rolling green hills, Don pointed out the new haberdashery shop that had opened and suggested that Madame may like to pop in to admire the new season's bonnets. Evelyn said they might have a look through the window, where the board games and puzzles in the Mind Games store morphed into pretty bonnets and reams of ribbon and cotton.

'Do you sew, Madame?' Don asked in a posh English accent.

'It's a desirable skill in a woman, but I focus on the pianola,' Evelyn said. She enjoyed this role-play and pondered, perhaps, that she would have been more suited to days gone by. But when she realised she would have been a washer woman rather than a woman of leisure, she decided she was happy where she was. Sir and Madame discussed local politics, with the odd shooing away of imaginary Dickensian child beggars as they meandered their way to the park. Evelyn reminded herself to drink slowly. When things were going so swimmingly, it was important to keep a firm head.

When they reached the park, they unhooked their arms without anyone going first, and turned their attention to the ground for an appropriate stick. The accents were gone, they were back in their painting clothes and their surrounds became familiar again. Don found the best stick, along with an acceptable backup stick, and they headed back to the laundromat. Dusk disappeared fast as they walked, and the darkness settled in around them. Evelyn did so love this time of day. Almost as much as mornings. There was an easy silence as their boots clomped along the asphalt.

CHAPTER SIX

*O*n returning to the laundromat, Don rubbed the sticks between his palms vigorously. He did a thorough job, and by the time the best stick entered the paint, which was not the blue fire engines would be if fire engines were blue, there was no way any stray piece of leaf, bark or sliver of stick skin would errantly find its way into the thick paint. Evelyn fluffed her rags and made sure no loose lint would sully the paint either. Don nodded appreciatively as she did this in the far corner of the room. He had bought a small knapsack with him and explained that, although Evelyn had all the required items, he would prefer to use his own brushes and rollers. To hide her discontent, she offered to heat up some party pies. Don said party pies were suitable fodder for a painting party.

'It might reduce my wine wooziness,' he said, swanning around like he was more drunk than he was. Evelyn thought he would make a fine hobo but chose not to say so. In fact, she was quite proud of herself that evening. She couldn't remember showing such restraint in the near distant past. This very lack of restraint had singlehandedly ruined her previous lives, but obviously she had learned her lesson and her life as a businesswoman was a wonderful new existence. If nothing else, Evelyn had learned to turn over new leaves in spectacular fashion. Not a single person had ever made it into any of her new lives. Not even an accidental sighting – thanks to Evelyn's highly tuned situational awareness.

She managed to lose some time in her kitchenette as she pondered herself, and she was embarrassed when she came back into the main room. Don didn't say a word about her long absence, nor display a particle of curiosity when she sashayed back in with the party pies. He had been solely focused on the job at hand and the wall now had its first coat. He smiled casually when she returned, and they both sat at the formica table and ate their party pies. As Evelyn chatted away about the neighbourhood, she made sure to keep things informative only, because no one likes a gossip. When they were done, she offered to cut in the next coat from the opposite side.

'Cutting in requires the same hand. No matter how subtle the difference, it would show,' he said as he climbed the ladder and began the line across the ceiling. Evelyn liked his way of explaining things. It was never condescending, which, if truth be told, most people were. He was logical and had an admirable brevity about his conversation. This pleased Evelyn no end, for as much as her feet were firmly placed on the ground, her head was as steadfastly melded into the clouds. Don was providing some much-needed change from the same old daydreams and mental follies that she had done and redone so many times they were now fermented pulp. Don was new fodder. She leaned back in her chair, had a large sip of wine and watched him work as she let her mind wander.

As a natural extension of their real-life walk, sashaying along in imaginary olden-day Britain, Evelyn pictured them both sitting at Lord's. It was the fifth day of the test and victory was within the grasp of both teams. They were sitting under a verandah in the fancy section, with mini sandwiches in one hand and a champagne flute in the other. They were in each other's worlds and eyes and hearts; passers-by smiled and nodded at this most enviable couple – after all, who wouldn't want to be them? Right out of the blue, the Australian captain hit a massive six to win the match and Evelyn stuck out her arm and caught the ball seamlessly to thunderous applause, with no outside sign that the tendons in her palm had been ripped open. The image was so lifelike that her hand hurt, and she stood suddenly and stared ahead.

In the laundromat, actual Don had the sense not to ask if she was okay. He just glanced at her briefly with that annoying crooked goofy smile and asked for another glass of wine, if it wasn't too much trouble. Evelyn put on quite the show, pouring his wine and rambling about the number of things on her to-do list to mask that she had been in faraway lands. Bless the man, he even asked if there was anything he could do to help. She dismissed his offer and said she was quite happy sitting there like the Queen of England while her staff painted her wall. He grinned broadly and bowed so low she hoped he didn't put his back out. If nothing else, he had a lovely sense of play. She curtsied and went to fetch another bottle of wine. Again, her act of following Don not quite home was justified. If she hadn't, they would have run out of wine.

As she flicked the lid into the bin, she found herself in the delightful stage of drinking. Her inhibitions were flying outside in the night sky, too far away for her to see them, and her sensibilities floated about above her head. She was not in the danger zone yet and she waltzed back into the room to hand Don a fresh glass. He said his old glass was fine, but she pooh-poohed him away and remarked that washing ten dishes was the same as washing one. They stood back and looked at the cutting in with analytical eyes.

Don filled the roller tray with the rich blue, which Evelyn quite liked now, even though it was still a little dark and dusty for her liking. They clinked glasses and Don told her all about his badminton team as he rolled. They were leading the season in D grade, and he boasted that next season they would elevate themselves to C grade, not that it mattered. When he spoke of his unexpected run back to the baseline and an overhead blind shot that just missed the reach of a six-foot-two young, agile opponent, Evelyn made a mental note that next time she and Don went to her imaginary cricket game, they would sit in the less fancy section (where the people would be just as admiring of their outward once-in-a-lifetime connection) as it just wasn't feasible for any cricketer to hit a big enough six to land in the fancy section. The thing with dreams is they have to have a foot in reality, and Evelyn admonished herself for such a beginner's oversight. Still, fixing dreams was the fun bit and she smiled to herself, which Don saw as interest in his badminton plays. So he continued to list his achievements, with slight embellishments.

At some point Evelyn actually listened and commented on his clever life choices. It was important, after all, to have hobbies and interests and to put oneself out there and take a chance by joining a club. She told him about the time she joined a choir for the same reasons. It had not gone well, because she couldn't sing in tune to save her life. Evelyn and Don launched into a version of 'Bohemian Rhapsody' at the top of their lungs. Evelyn threw her head back and committed. They went for as long as they knew the lyrics and, as the song faded, the second horizontal coat was complete. It also received a few moments of appreciation.

Evelyn noted to herself that she was entering the drinking danger zone. It was definitely the time of risk. Where unintended words are uttered, where the shields are too low. While Don began cutting in again, she went to the kitchenette and poured them both a large glass of water.

During this last phase of painting, Don made the mistake of asking about Evelyn's past. She noted that the queries had been casual, not intrusive, and shunted his questions. To deflect, she asked him about his past, and he babbled about his family tree, blissfully unaware that she was not listening. She was up in a hot air balloon with Don, who had trimmed his goatee, and they were admiring the rolling green hills of the peninsula. Just as the balloon was too low and possibly about to hit a rather beautiful white ghost gum tree, he asked whether she had seen the new *Bohemian Rhapsody* movie. She looked over at him blankly and asked him to repeat the last sentence. He did.

'No, not yet,' Evelyn said, before saying how much she liked seeing films on the big screen at the cinema. He casually mentioned that perhaps they should go and see it together. Evelyn wondered just how the conversation had got to this point before saying she was open to it. After all, the more she got to know Don, the better her dreams would be.

Evelyn looked at her watch and groaned internally. It was getting late and she felt a little overwhelmed at the dishes, the dirty paint items, the smell of the not dried paint, the day ahead. The water had been a good idea, but it had taken the gloss off her reverie. Her inhibitions had flown back inside her body and a dull thump started at the back of her forehead. But she pulled herself together and smiled admiringly at the finished wall with Don before she hurriedly said he'd best be off and leave her to sort out what needed to be done.

Evelyn made it clear she was grateful for her new wall and walked Don to the front door. Her thanks were genuine, and appreciated, and she waved him off as he headed down the street. She stayed there until he was out of sight. A good thing too, because he had looked over his shoulder twice, and it just wouldn't do to have him see an empty path.

As she waved, she saw herself farewelling a uniformed Don heading off to help the government who needed his scientific brain to decode enemy messages. Then she went back inside and fine-tuned her balloon trip, his natural skills at decoding, which had impressed a team of experts, and moved their position at Lord's to the boundary fence as she cleaned up before flopping her heavy head onto the pillow for a fitful night ahead.

CHAPTER SEVEN

*E*velyn awoke with a dreadful fog in her brain; the downside to frolicking around with a bellyful of wine. When the alarm went off, she nearly cried, but she refrained and swung her leaden legs out of bed. She chose coffee and her morning routine over extra lie down time in bed. It wouldn't be significantly beneficial anyway. She barely smiled at the miserable coffee couple, and she was surprised to find the coffee didn't help lift her mood at all. Not one bit. In fact, it was like drinking sand. Bitter, eyewatering sand, yet she finished it.

Rather than taking a stroll in the park, she walked back to the laundromat and pottered around her office. As she stood at her ironing board, she became morose. Today, her usual journeys to other lands bore no reward. Every time she tried her imaginings, they felt futile. Even the old stalwarts had no legs. Her hangover decimated them and left her standing there – a maudlin woman without purpose in a pile of insurmountable minutes. It was going to be a long day. Even opening the door and letting the day in, which normally filled her with anticipation, was just a reminder that hours of drudgery awaited.

Evelyn pushed her nausea down to the bottom of her boots and tried to shake away the cloud in her head. It felt like her shrunken brain was rattling around inside her skull and she reminded herself to restrict and slow all movement. She tried not to fall into the hangover trap of thinking that food solves all ills, and battled through to lunchtime when she popped over to the bakery. The pie was muddy, and the lamington was dry, hard work, but her head had cleared enough to see herself watching a sunset with Don atop a cliff. The other couples barbequing nearby all looked at them with envy as she ironed away. At four o'clock, she was most surprised to hear Ben calling out for her.

'Evie, are you here?' he said, popping his head over the bottom half of her stable-style door.

'Young Ben,' she said, her delight in no way feigned. She smoothed his hair and said, 'It's not Tuesday.' Then she asked where his mother was. His big eyes welled up with tears and he blinked them away as quickly as they had arrived. The effort to not cry was taking so much of his strength that his words got stuck. Rather than force the issue, Evelyn opened her door and went out to sit at the formica table. Ben followed and sat down too. Evelyn explained that he was such a good and responsible young man that she was going to close the laundromat door, put up the 'Back in five minutes' sign and run out the back to make him some toast and get him a glass of milk.

'Because a little bit of toast and a drink of milk always helps when there's trouble afoot,' she said, standing up decisively and setting off to do what she'd said. The toast seemed to take forever as she mulled over what could possibly be wrong with the young fellow. Her heart was racing as all the disastrous situations ran through her mind like Olympic sprinters. By the time she returned to Ben with toast and milk, she had worked herself up into a lather. Then her phone pinged with a message.

'Oh for god's sake,' she said after she had read it, shook her head and put the phone back in her pinny pocket.

'What's wrong, Evie?' Ben said, his forehead crinkled in concern.

'Oh nothing dear, just someone telling me they hoped I had a nice day.' She waved dismissively.

'I think that's nice,' Ben said, looking a little confused.

'Well, I guess it could look that way, but it's such a waste of time, you see, and now all I can think about is a stupid message that wasted my time and now more time is wasted.' Evelyn realised how she sounded, even though she was right. The message had already taken up too much of her mind space, so she withdrew from giving the boy a lesson in effective communication and put his food down in front of him.

Ben picked at it and moved the toast squares around the plate. It was not the normal greedy guts approach he took to food and Evelyn used all her resolve not to force a conversation. Instead, she waited. After a minute, Ben explained he had lost his key somewhere at school and that he hadn't been able to get inside when he got home and, even though he knocked, no one was home to answer the door.

'Well, sometimes grown-ups have grown-up things to do, and maybe your mum is running a little late,' Evelyn said, to set his mind at ease – and to pry as to whether his mother was often absent when he got home. He seemed too little to be left home alone, but Evelyn wasn't an expert in these things. Ben explained sometimes his mum was home and sometimes she wasn't, but that she always left a note when she wasn't there.

'And she comes home when it says on the note,' Ben said, nodding his head. 'Well, mostly,' he added as he put a crust in his mouth. He was on a roll now, and he had cheered up somewhat. Evelyn didn't want Ben to know that she knew where he lived, but she had certainly been justified in following them home a few months ago . . . in case something happened. Because something had happened.

Ben acted like she had insulted his intelligence when she asked whether he knew how to get home. Evelyn said that he could hang around with her until five o'clock and they would head over to his house together. She stood up and invited Ben out the back with her.

Evelyn gave Ben a tutorial on how to best iron a shirt because, before he knew it, he would be working and would need to know how to do it properly. After Ben washed his hands, and Evelyn inspected both sides of them, he was allowed to help. As they ironed, she hung the shirts on the rack and young Ben did up the buttons. He was slow, but methodical, and Evelyn respected how seriously he took the job. He did it so well that there were no wrinkles around the buttons, so she wouldn't have to do them all over again when he had gone home. In between, she emptied the coin boxes on the washing machines and set him up to place twenty one-dollar coins in each mini bank bag.

'Not nineteen, and not twenty-one,' she said, to be doubly sure. Ben counted out the coins slowly and did a very good job. Evelyn watched out of the corner of her eye and decided he was going to be a fine adult at the end of his long childhood. For a moment, Ben went to the cricket with Don and Evelyn, sitting right in the middle with both their arms around him. Just as she was about to go to Ben's school concert in her mind, with Ben being the star of the show and all the teachers fussing over the relatives, her alarm went off. It was time to shut up shop. She asked him to wait right there while she ran upstairs to get a couple of things.

Evelyn went to the third drawer down in her dresser. It was her drawer of things past. Nothing from her past was on display, but she had one item from each of her previous lives. Never two. She felt no emotion when she opened the drawer, she simply grabbed a black leather oblong case that would almost fit a pair of glasses inside. There was a thick brass zip going around three of the four sides and she opened it to check everything she needed was inside. She zipped it back up and put it in her tote bag. Finally, she put a green jumper on and headed back downstairs to collect Ben; her hangover pushed firmly into the 'I will not acknowledge you' pigeonhole.

When she got downstairs, Ben was shifting uneasily. Evelyn knew he was doubting his choice to come to her. She ignored his doubt and took charge. It was time to go, but perhaps he would like to stop off quickly for some more food? Now he was really torn. Belly versus trouble. He went for the belly.

At the local fish and chip shop, they sat down on the vinyl chairs to wait. It was time to upgrade the laundromat chairs, Evelyn decided. When she mentioned this to Ben, he seemed uninterested, but Evelyn pushed forward and asked whether he'd like to help her pick some new ones one day.

'I'd rather go to the zoo,' he said, 'I never get to go to the zoo.' Evelyn bumped her shoulder on his and jutted her chin towards the fish and chip man, who shook the oil from the wire basket and plopped their food out onto some crisp white paper. The man looked at Evelyn, salt shaker in hand. She couldn't remember when salt became optional. It used to be a given.

'Can we have chicken salt, please?' Ben asked, his eyes lighting up for the first time that day. Evelyn nodded at the fish and chip man, even though she didn't like chicken salt. Chicken and fish don't go together.

She had been mildly curious about the new owners of the fish and chip shop and had noted that she could hear children from behind the curtain separating the shop from the personal quarters. She liked that it was a family business because busy parents meant the kids had to amuse themselves to an extent. And that was much better than having hovering adults living vicariously through them.

'Pickled onion, Ben?' Evelyn asked. He screwed up his nose and shook his head. Evelyn liked a pickled onion. It got right up her nose and cleared her brain, so she got one for herself. She saved introducing herself to the fish and chip shop man, as she had more important things to do, but finding out more about the new family was now firmly on her mental to-do list.

Evelyn and Ben set off, and she made sure to stay a little behind him, so he thought she was following him. When he cut through the park, she suggested a wee sit. Ben sat on Evelyn's bench, and they ploughed their way through some chips. Ben was listing all his favourite animals. The nice young man was throwing a ball for Nutmeg, and Evelyn waved at him and held up the chips. The man wandered over and introduced himself to Ben while Nutmeg sat restlessly by his side. Nutmeg knew the rules, but he could barely keep his bum on the ground, and he wriggled just off the grass with a helicoptering tail. The smell of the food, the sight of the ball was almost too much.

'Can I give him a chip?' Ben asked as he looked longingly at the chestnut brown curly-topped dog. The nice man debated this briefly and decided that the happiness of the boy outweighed the poor dietary choice for the mutt. Ben flew off the bench and gave the dog a chip, who took it gently yet enthusiastically from his hand. Ben grinned and patted the dog. The nice man gave him the ball and Ben started throwing it with all his might, the food a long distant memory. The man told Evelyn he'd moved into the area a few months back and got himself a dog for therapy. He'd been through a breakup and decided it was time for a new start. Evelyn asked what he did with his time, which was more polite than asking what he did for a living, and he said he was in between jobs. Evelyn didn't like people in between jobs, because it usually meant they were lazy, so she took her leave and called to Ben. Unemployed father figures are no good for a young man so she said goodbye icily. The man didn't seem to notice her disdain and waved happily as they left.

Evelyn followed Ben to the apartment block next to the one the forgetful man with a beige suit lived in. The front door was propped open with a brick, which rankled Evelyn. A distinct lack of security right there. She followed Ben up a flight of stairs, and he stood outside the left-hand apartment off the landing. He proceeded to double-check his pockets and bag for his key, getting more and more fraught as the seconds ticked by. Evelyn told Ben she had magic powers that only worked if no one was looking. She asked him to turn around, close his eyes and count to twenty. Like they were playing a game of hide and seek.

After he had turned and squeezed his eyes very shut, she took the leather pouch from her pocket and examined the lock. It was basic. She chose two lockpicking tools and placed a long straight metal strip into the barrel. It helped her guide the hooked piece, which she raked across the pins. One by one, she pushed them up, longest to shortest, and as the last one clicked up, the latch gave way. As Ben reached twelve, she secreted her tools and held the door ajar. When he turned around, he looked up at her like she was a magician.

'How did you do that?' he asked.

Evelyn said if she spoke of the magic, the magic would never work again, then waited. What happened next wasn't up to her. Ben pushed the door open, ran into the kitchen to the right, then ran out to the lounge room. Evelyn couldn't see much of it, but there was a corner of a bed visible. It was a one-bedroom flat, and Ben's mum clearly slept in the lounge room. Ben scoured the place and came back to Evelyn with a note clutched in his hand.

'Mum say she'll be back by six,' he said as relief flowed down his face.

'What about your key problem?' Evelyn asked casually.

Ben took off again, giving Evelyn time to step into the doorway and analyse the flat. The kitchen floor was scattered with food, the benches hadn't been wiped for a few days, and there was a pile of dishes at the sink. This was good and bad. Good because clearly food was being prepared, bad because the hygiene standards were appalling. She poked her head into the lounge/bedroom and saw that the bed had the covers pulled up. Not quite made, but at least Ben's mum had gone to the effort of almost making it. The place didn't smell of smoke, and her clothes had been put in stacks of milk crates lined up under the bed, with the open ends facing out. One of them contained sketch pads and pencils, and Evelyn felt relieved that the woman had a hobby. She thought the storage system quite imaginative and supposed the milk crates created a solid bed base, if you didn't have one. She got back to the front door just as Ben ran over to her, holding up a key like it was treasure.

'I just forgot it, Evie,' he said, smiling at her.

'What the fuck are you doing here?' Ben's mum's voice said from behind them. Evelyn heard the menace of years of pent-up anger in the woman's tone and stood very still.

'Hello, dear,' she said, turning to face Ben's mother. Even tone, big smile, act as though it was perfectly normal to find your local laundromat lady in your doorway. Ben's mum stepped into Evelyn's space and put her face right up to hers.

'You see, I was visiting a friend in the next block; you might have seen him around. An older chap in a beige suit?'

Evelyn began, 'and lo and behold I saw young Ben here outside your building, so I came over to say hi.' Ben's mother was not sold. 'We got to chatting and before I knew it, I was standing here.' She would have put her hands out in a ta-da, what-do-you-know way, but Ben's mum was still right in her face. When in doubt, keep talking.

Evelyn explained that they were chatting about animals, that she loved going to the zoo, how lovely it would be if she had some company. Perhaps, she suggested, Ben would like to go to the zoo on Sunday.

'You could come too,' Evelyn said in her most pleasant and amiable way. But her insides were steel.

Ben's mum face did not soften one iota, but she did step sideways slightly. Evelyn followed her lead and slowly they pirouetted separately together, then Ben's mum stepped inside her doorway. She muttered something about strangers, and Ben said Evie wasn't even a stranger. Ben's mum deflated a little, and murderous became couldn't give a fuck.

'Anyway, tomorrow's Tuesday, so I'll see you at the laundromat,' Evelyn said as she turned to leave. 'You can have a think about the zoo in the meantime,' she said over her shoulder as she waved.

The door had slammed halfway through her sentence, but never mind. Evelyn's heart was racing, her face was flushed, and her breaths were laboured as she made her way down the stairs. The whole interaction had been a bit of a shock, and her hands shook just a little as she patted her pockets to make sure she had all her things. She supposed she would have acted the same way if the shoe had been on the other foot, and decided to have a little sit on the low brick fence outside the block of units to recalibrate.

Unusually, Evelyn barely noticed the twenty-something girl smoking on the nature strip. Normally she would proffer a scowl, but not this time. It wasn't until another twenty-something exited Phillip's neighbouring apartment block that she noticed the two of them and how on edge they seemed.

'She's not answering,' the second girl said, glancing back at the building anxiously.

Ben's mum's menacing ways left Evelyn's mind and she immediately tuned in to the problem the two women faced. Perhaps she could help.

'This is not right,' the smoker said, shaking her head. 'Do you think we should go to the police?'

Evelyn held herself still so her interest didn't rear its head and interrupt.

'What for? It's not like they'll give a fuck,' the other one said, fishing through her handbag. 'We'll see if she comes tomorrow night. If she misses two weeks, we'll do it.' She clicked her key fob and they headed over to a tired looking Toyota.

'Home game?' the smoker girl asked as she opened the passenger door of the car.

'Nuh, we're playing the shooters at the station.'

Evelyn stood as the car drove up the street and wondered what the shooters at the station could be.

CHAPTER EIGHT

*E*velyn had a tick day. Everything just fell into place, from the moment the coffee cart couple smiled at her at the break of dawn. She delighted in seeing them so relaxed and their brief chat, even if it was just about the weather, boosted the prospects of Evelyn's upcoming day. When she sat on the park bench, Nutmeg ran over and sniffed her knee like it held the key to the mysteries of the world. The custard tart she got for morning tea was slightly overbaked, which was just how she liked them. Crispy, crumbly, almost smoked pastry gave the perfectly set custard some texture, and she held each mouthful for a few extra seconds and breathed in over the yummy mess in her mouth to accentuate the flavour as she stood looking out her front window.

Tattoo Man and Ash were walking down the other side of the street, and he was so busy gesticulating about the most important thing in the universe that he didn't see the 'No Standing' pole. When he walked straight into it, Evelyn spat out a gelatinous mouthful as an uncontainable giggle fit took hold. As she cleaned the inside of her window, she admonished herself for finding mirth in the misfortune of others. Self-forgiveness came quickly though. Had he been hurt, as opposed to shocked, of course she would have rushed to help instead of laughing to her core.

Evelyn wondered, on and off, whether Ben and his mum would come in for Washing Day Tuesday and figured they would, despite the feisty interaction the previous evening. Because tick days are tick days. If only they were predictable, she mused, then she could save up all the little things for the days where everything goes right.

By the time Ben rushed into the laundromat, Evelyn realised that time had slipped away and there were no bakery goods for him. She took five dollars out of her register and asked him if he would be a dear and go on her behalf, as she had been too busy to do it herself. It was important to backtrack to the pedestrian crossing, safety first, and make sure he said please and thank you to Cheryl, who was such a nice lady. He could take his pick from the specials and choose something for her as well, as she wasn't a fusspot. Which wasn't entirely true. She did not like pasties. At all.

'I better ask my mum if I can go,' he said as he dumped his school bag at her stable-style door. He said this just as his mother walked in with the weight of the world on her shoulders. 'Evie asked me to go to the bakery for her because she's been very busy,' he said to his mum. He seemed to calculate the distance between them. Too close meant no; so did too far away. The sweet zone. His mum shrugged agreement and loaded the machine. Evelyn waited as long as she could before she spoke.

'I'm sorry I gave you a fright last night, dear,' she said casually, 'I didn't mean any harm.' The woman shrugged again. Perhaps she was too tired to speak. 'Anyway, I'm sure young Ben would love to come to the zoo on Sunday. It would be nice to have some company while I walk around.' She'd just finished speaking when Ben rushed in with two paper bags.

'You can take him if you want,' Ben's mother said dismissively. Well, Evelyn could hardly believe her luck, and Ben froze with his mouth open for a moment.

By the time their washing had finished, arrangements were set. Evelyn would pick him up at nine so they could get there just as the doors opened. Ben had barely touched his food as he babbled about all the animals they'd see. He skipped out the door ahead of his mother who had the grace to look back around at Evelyn and nod in thanks.

'I'm June, by the way. I'm also fuckin' tired,' she said over her shoulder as they left. Evelyn liked that she felt the need to justify her nonchalance and her inability to engage. Evelyn shrugged in response – when in Rome.

When Evelyn closed the laundromat, she strolled down to The Station Hotel and stopped to admire it for a moment. It was a three-storey dame painted a dusty light blue with maroon trims. She had chosen to wear jeans, her old well-loved green shoes (the green fire engines would be if fire engines were green), a casual button-up shirt and a silky golden headscarf. A bit of everything; in case she had to be a bit of everything. She sat by a window at the pub so she could see the street, the hallway that led to the bistro and the pool tables at the back of the public bar. Evelyn was prone to dropping in to the pub for the occasional trivia night, but she hadn't been for a while.

One trivia night, she had gone to the bathroom and seen someone call a friend and whisper the question down the phone. Cheating. Evelyn hadn't quite known what to do. Cheating should be called out, but the thickset brunette looked like she would savour a fight, so Evelyn chose to shut her mouth. When she returned to her team, called The Misfits because they had all come alone, she informed them of the appalling behaviour. No one else on her team had cared, and she couldn't believe it. One man, whose fingernails looked like they had nine years of grime under them, said they were there for fun and not to worry about it.

'Fun?' Evelyn had said rather too loudly. She had feigned a headache two questions into the music round, made her leave and had not returned to trivia night since, although it would be fun to go with Don.

After two slow wines – it was important for her to be on her toes – she watched as a group of women slowly built up around the pool tables. They seemed haphazard at first. A sturdy jolly woman wearing red corduroy pants with a wild set of springy Tigger tail curls entered with a pointy-chinned thin woman twice her age. The pointy woman darted her face around at all things irrelevant. If Evelyn was looking around at a room, she would look at the people and the exits, whereas the pointy woman looked under tables and examined the ceiling forensically. Next came a serious woman with helmet hair whose jeans were too tight. She wore wire-rimmed glasses with such a strong prescription that her eyes almost filled the lenses. Unlike the pointy woman, she looked at sensible places and clocked everyone in the room, including Evelyn, who put on her nonchalant face and produced the briefest of nods when she caught her enlarged eyes. The two young girls from the previous evening came next, looking anxiously around the room for their friend. Nothing. They stood around one end of the pool room, each buying a drink, before being joined by a tall woman who looked like nothing had piqued her interest in decades. Evelyn heard the group talking about being a player down, and the serious helmet-haired woman looked even more unhappy than she had when she'd entered. Evelyn moved tables to be closer to the game.

A new group of women entered, two at a time. Evelyn hummed 'The animals come in two by two, hurrah, hurrah,' and knew the catchy ditty would not leave her head for days. There was only one way to get rid of a persistent head tune, and that was to spread the contagion as far and wide as possible. The more people who caught it, minimum of six, the sooner it would exit her head. When she went to get a drink, the barmaid asked her which song she was humming. It reminded her of something, she said as she poured the wine. Evelyn said she didn't know but her teeth felt furry. The barmaid looked at her like she was a specimen on a microscope glass for a second then was distracted by the two girls who came up for a drink. Evelyn smiled at them and said they looked a little distressed, a little tired. The girls said they'd had better days.

'Well, every day's a better day until it isn't,' Evelyn said. One girl smiled, the other did not. Evelyn returned to her table to watch, listen and learn. It was the second week that the team were a player down. The other players were much more interested in feeling aggrieved than concerned for their missing teammate. The helmet-haired woman said that this would never have happened when she had been secretary of the league. For Evelyn, the pieces started falling into place. The helmet-haired woman clearly felt that the missing girl should never have been given the league's organisational role, as she had done such a good job herself since the league's inception. But Evelyn could clearly see why the helmet-haired woman had been usurped. She was unpleasant and clearly did things her way, and her way only.

The two girls were bearing the blame, not just for the forfeiture of the games two weeks running, but for all the helmet-haired woman's ills. This included the missing floral tin that held all the league's paperwork, banking deposit books and any money yet to be banked. It had belonged to the helmet-haired woman's grandmother and held high sentimental value. The end of the season was nigh, and even the second team began complaining when they discussed that the end of year celebration was not only upcoming, but that the venue was waiting for payment to hire out the function room. The man who made the trophies was also waiting for his deposit. The two girls seemed to get smaller and smaller in their chairs, and when the time came for their games, they could barely pot a ball – which exacerbated the helmet-haired woman's frustrations with them.

At the halfway mark, a break was called, and Evelyn timed her trip to the bar so she was standing next to the two girls again. Evelyn explained that she wasn't normally an eavesdropper, but it had been hard to miss their plight and the tension in the air.

'I heard you say your friend was missing,' she added casually. 'My name's Evelyn, I run a local business up the road.' Evelyn made sure to keep her face somewhere between caring, concerned and wise.

'Yeah, no one is treating us seriously, but we know something's wrong,' the round-faced girl said as she picked at a coaster. When the drinks were put down in front of them, Evelyn paid. Both girls said thank you. The small gesture had visibly warmed their hearts.

'Have you been to the police station?' Evelyn asked.

'Yeah, they don't give a shit,' the round-faced girl said as despondency washed through her chocolate brown eyes.

'Does she live locally, maybe I've seen her around?' The girls pepped up a little and the round-faced girl introduced them both as they searched through their phones for a good picture. Her name was Andy; the quieter girl with the naturally sceptical face was Molly. Evelyn looked at a picture on Molly's phone and said the missing girl had been into her laundromat to ask about dry-cleaning, which wasn't part of Evelyn's business, and she had directed her to the dry-cleaner in the sad strip of shops at Wattle Grove, near Don's. 'Have you knocked on doors around her house?' Evelyn asked.

'Oh, like in the movies . . . Hey, Molly,' Andy said, forgetting Evelyn was there for a moment, 'we could canvas the neighbourhood!' She slapped the bar as she spoke.

'I could help,' Evelyn said, keeping the enthusiasm out of her tone. She didn't want to come on too strong.

Both girls looked at her like she was a mouldy apple, but Evelyn was not deterred. 'It will be quicker if we divide up the neighbourhood between us. All you need to do is print out photos beforehand,' Evelyn said. If nothing else, she was persistent. She explained where the laundromat was, said she was free after she closed up shop the following night if they were interested in an extra set of hands.

The seed was planted, now she just had to wait. The games resumed, and Evelyn stayed for one more drink. The girls whispered to themselves from time to time and glanced over at Evelyn twice, which convinced her that they would turn up the following day. After all, today was a tick day.

CHAPTER NINE

*T*he girls did turn up. Just as Evelyn was closing for the day, the old silver Toyota pulled up and the girls waved to her. Evelyn felt excited, then checked herself. Their friend was missing, and it wouldn't do to be overly enthusiastic. The three of them had a brief discussion, and it was decided that the doorknock would involve the two apartment blocks on the other side of the park. The missing girl, Dee, lived on the second floor in the same building as the forgetful old man with the beige suit.

'I'll take this building,' Evelyn said with authority when they faced the buildings. She wanted to avoid knocking on June and Ben's door in the neighbouring apartment block, and this way she could check on the old man in apartment three. Molly had brought some A4 sheets of paper with the missing girl's name and picture on them. There were two phone numbers as well. Evelyn suggested they put some up on the light poles, like people do when they can't find their pets. Andy had embraced the idea; Molly said Dee was a person, not a dog or cat, but had agreed in the end. But first things first.

Evelyn gave each of the girls a notepad and suggested they make a list of any units that didn't answer so they could go back if need be. Then she headed into her apartment block and made her way straight up to the top. Easier to work downwards, she figured. Like doing the sky first in a jigsaw puzzle. Hard bits first made the rest easier.

As she climbed the stairs, she practised her kindest face and sweetest smile, designed to allay fears. By the time she completed the top floor, there had been only one person who recognised the girl. It was the nice man who walked Nutmeg. He said she had loved his dog and patted him every time they crossed paths, but that he hadn't seen her for what must have been at least a week. She had no joy at all on the second floor, but a watery-eyed lady in her eighties had asked if she would like a cup of tea, seeing as it must be so upsetting losing someone. Evelyn asked for water instead and stepped into an immaculately kept time capsule.

'Oh, what a lovely family you have,' Evelyn said encouragingly when the lady brought her a glass of water in shaky hands. The old lady looked at the photo and said it came with the frame. Evelyn welled up and willed her tears away. It was a combination of vicarious feelings, and thinking that perhaps she ought to buy a frame with a pre-existing family so she didn't feel so alone either. By the time she got to the bottom floor, she had decided that doorknocking was not what she thought it would be. She thought she would have pages full of notes and a trail of information that led to X marks the spot.

Evelyn stood at the door where the old man in the beige suit lived and rapped loudly in case he was hard of hearing. When he answered the door, he looked at her blankly for a moment before recognition flowed down his face.

'Hello, have you seen this girl?' Evelyn asked, holding up the photo. He looked closely at it, which she appreciated. Evelyn had always taken the time to give any question she was asked some thought. To give the illusion that she was giving it due consideration, even if she had predetermined her answer. It was one of the things that made her likeable.

'No. Go to the police station and get an L18 form filled out,' he said as he closed the door. Evelyn stuck out a well-practised foot. While ironing one day, she had moved her foot out over and over again in case of this eventuality, and she just saved the door from closing in her face.

'Excuse me, sir,' she said, 'what is an L18?' She kept her tone neutral and swallowed her curiosity. Desperation was always a spanner in her workings.

'Missing persons form,' he said with a shrug. He then turned and walked inside. As he hadn't shut the door, she decided it was an invitation to enter. The foyer was small and made even smaller by the stacks of books and newspapers on nearly all available floor space. When she walked into the lounge room, she was most delighted to find a miniature train set that took up the whole room bar a walkway to what would be the kitchen one way and a bedroom the other. She stood there watching a train go over hills and down dales, past a matchstick tree forest with green cotton-wool canopies. There was a wee village, a suspension bridge and men in overalls along the tracks sporting pickaxes and shovels. One man had no tools but stood in front of a line of men in striped overalls, each with a different criminal number on the back of their jerseys. She could have sworn she saw sweat on their faces. The village houses had thatched rooves, some lit inside, and the occasional farmer tilled the nearby fields. She felt the wind in her hair as Mini Evelyn sat on the sills of the steam train with her feet hanging over the edge. When a stray piece of coke flew into her eye, she rubbed it vigorously. She gazed down over the river as the train crossed the bridge and looked forward to getting home to her little cottage.

The fire was already stoked, and she was keen to share news from her day at the local markets with her partner, who was currently picking fresh carrots from the veggie patch. Evelyn tore herself away from her reverie and went into the kitchen – she had work to do. She stood in the doorway and fake coughed to get the old man's attention. He was clearly startled as he turned away from his small pot on the stove and his eyes became steely.

'How do you know what an L18 is?' Evelyn asked, hoping that a continuance in conversation would remind him that she wasn't a stranger.

'I was a policeman for many years,' he said, turning back to his pot. Evelyn could smell baked beans and pushed the disgust from her face. She'd rather eat toenails.

'Well, that's amazing, thank you for your service,' she said. She didn't recall ever meeting a policeman before, except for the time someone had tried to break into the laundromat. The streetlight outside the door illuminated those outside, so if all her lights were out, she could see them, but they couldn't see her. There had been a man jiggling her lock, and she had slipped out the back to get a hammer from her toolbox. She had crept right up to the door and stood with the hammer raised like she would have at the fair if she had been trying to win a teddy bear by smashing the mallet down on a pressure pad, which would then push the dinger up the stick towards the bell at the top. Evelyn had watched all manner of people at the fair once, and not one had managed to ding the elusive bell. She decided it was rigged and didn't spend a cent on trying to win at that game. When the robber had jiggled the lock open, she had smashed the hammer down on the hand that gripped the side of the door to push it open. The man had screamed gutturally, and Evelyn had rejoiced that she had hit her target.

'Ding, ding, I win the teddy bear,' she had shouted at the top of her lungs. The intruder had run away. When the police arrived to hear about the break-in, they had told her she had done the wrong thing. The intruder may have got the hammer off her and used it against her, and it was important not to engage with criminals. Evelyn was disappointed in the policeman, as she was half expecting a citizen medal for her efforts. Nothing had been taken and the whole episode had dissipated and ended with disappointment. She was sure this dignified old man would have verily pinned a medal on her chest if he had been the first responder instead.

The old man nodded briefly at her as he removed the pot from the stove and retrieved a bowl from the sink. It was clearly dirty, but, after a brief examination, he decided it was acceptable and flipped the pan upside down. Evelyn watched as the last beans slid their way down the silvery saucepan into the bowl.

'I bet you have some stories,' Evelyn said in her most inviting tone. He proceeded to tell her about the time he had attended a brothel. One of the girls had called up and said that one of the workers was wasted and walking around aggressively. When he had arrived on the scene, all the workers were out on the street shivering. It was cold, and he and his partner had entered the premises to remove the troublemaker. He said his gun had caught on the curtain just inside the door, and the whole curtain had come crashing down. The girl had heard the ruckus, picked up the curtain rod and had chased the two policemen around the brothel until they managed to contain her and remove her from the premises. The old man laughed deeply as he finished his tale, and Evelyn was beaming. 'What a terrific story,' she said. He became contemplative and stared at his beans.

'I try not to remember all the dead,' he said as his eyes drifted away into past worlds.

'Yes, well that's a mighty train set you have out there, did you build it yourself?' Evelyn didn't want to remember his dead either. They walked over and stood there watching the train go around. He ate his baked beans while Mini Evelyn arrived home at her cottage, put her heavy market shopping bags on the table and was swept up in the arms of her lover. Mini Evelyn knew how to be loved.

'I don't suppose you'd come to the police station with us?' she asked, before explaining how tortured the two lovely girls were about their missing friend. 'Perhaps your being there would add some . . .' Evelyn stopped to block Mini Evelyn from returning to her head, 'legitimacy.' Not quite, but it would do. She was thrilled to find him agreeable and said she would go and tell the girls that they could all venture to the police station together.

CHAPTER TEN

*E*velyn briefed the girls, pooh-poohed Molly's scepticism and raced back inside to pick up the old man. When she got to his door, he was wrapping a grubby scarf around his neck with one hand and patting his pockets for his key with the other. Evelyn waited patiently on the outside while her insides auditioned for the whirling dervishes. She took the time to admire her self-restraint while he checked a hook on the doorframe. Her own history with keys was chequered. They were both surprised to find that his key was hanging there diligently and smiled warmly at each other. Those with key afflictions recognise each other innately.

Molly's scepticism returned as she looked the old man up and down. Even the ever-embracing Andy paused for a moment.

'This is,' Evelyn said, suddenly realising that she didn't know his name, 'our retired policeman.' Her ta-da finish went unacknowledged.

'I'm Phillip,' he said as he extended his hand formally to Molly. After introductions were complete, the foursome headed to the local police station. There was a brief stop when Phillip picked a daisy and performed the love-me, love-me-not ritual. He presented Evelyn with the stem, topped with a clearly embarrassed pistil and a sad, solitary petal which flapped about in the evening breeze. Apparently, he loved her not.

When they got to the shabby, square featureless building, the old man held the door open and they traipsed inside.

'Don't ring the bell,' he said authoritatively when Evelyn went to ding the bell.

'How will they know we're here?' she asked. The old man pointed at the mirror behind the counter and sat down on one of the plastic moulded chairs. They were all bolted together, and Evelyn wondered why. No one in their right mind would steal one. Phillip crossed his legs and clasped his hands behind his head. The two girls sat either side of him. Evelyn was not in the mood for sitting and wandered around the waiting room looking at the faded posters that looked like they'd been there for years. There was a chart of missing persons, and Evelyn vaguely remembered the tall cross-eyed man who had gone missing while bushwalking a few years back. They had never found him, as far as she knew.

After a while, the girls started shifting in their chairs. Andy got up and headed over to the bell.

'No,' Phillip said again. She asked why. He explained that they had no idea who had been before them and what sort of help they had needed. What if the person before them had been a woman with a black eye? What if a child had gone missing and the staff were all behind the mirror doing all they could to find them? He explained they needed to be patient and to kindly sit the fuck down and wait their turn. Even Evelyn sat down at that.

After a while, an older man with a moustache, a mustard stain on his chest and a perfectly round belly sitting above his low-slung belt wandered out into the foyer. He took his time checking his pockets for a pen and making sure the computer screen was on while he eyed the group.

Evelyn almost saw Phillip roll his eyes on the outside as he uncrossed and recrossed his legs. Now he was fighting to stay seated. The girls and Evelyn followed his lead and stayed put. Evelyn examined the policeman and thought he just might be the type to take longer if he was rushed and pulled a huge yawn in support of Phillip. The policeman jutted his chin forward at the old man and Phillip headed over to the counter. Evelyn and the girls followed.

'How can I help you?' the policeman asked, stifling a yawn. Evelyn wanted to tell him yawns were catchy, but she changed her mind.

'There's a girl missing, and we need to fill out an L18,' Phillip said. The policeman regarded the old man closely and straightened his posture a little.

'What's your number?' he asked. He still hadn't acknowledged that the others existed. Phillip mentioned a number in the seventy-six thousands, and Evelyn wished he had spoken slower so she could have remembered it. They back and forthed over where they had worked over the years, and they found a colleague in common. Apparently, he had moved down to Tasmania some time back. Evelyn listed twenty-six flavours of ice-cream in her head to contain herself and allow the banter to flow.

'Anyway, L18s don't exist anymore, old man,' the policeman said. 'It's all done on computer now,' he added, turning to the screen. Phillip nodded and introduced the girls to the policeman, who typed with two fingers. It was painful watching him take down the name and address of the missing girl.

'Are you family?' he asked.

'You don't have to be related to be family,' Evelyn said. Being helpful was one of her strengths. Phillip tugged at her shirt sleeve and eased her back a step from the group. Evelyn decided to file it away and take it up with him later.

By the time the questions were finished, it became clear to everyone that Andy and Molly knew very little about their friend, other than how funny and kind and clever she was. No names or contact details of family members, no knowledge of where she had come from, only a vague idea that her job involved something in finance or investing, and they didn't know of anyone who knew her before they met. Andy's eyes lit up when she remembered she had Dee's bank details, though. Surely that would help.

The foursome made their way back to the apartment block quietly. The girls were dejected, and Evelyn, unusually, had very little to say. She tried to pep them up with a joke, but it wasn't the right time, nor was it funny.

CHAPTER ELEVEN

*E*velyn and Phillip watched the girls get in their car and drive away. They both waved automatically, smiles plastered to their faces. When the car disappeared over the close horizon, they looked at each other and smiled at their ingrained manners. They had waved at the girls like they were relatives they wouldn't see until the same time next year.

Six and a half lifetimes ago, Evelyn had vowed never to see anyone on a once-a-year basis. To see someone just because that's what people did each festive season seemed futile. It wasn't a short enough time span to catch up on the minutiae of life – 'How's the ankle?' 'Did you get the job?' 'Is your partner still ignoring you for some minor infraction?' Instead, these visits inevitably led to uninvited trips down memory lane that highlighted only the moments she would rather forget. 'Oh wasn't it funny when –' No. 'Oh remember the time you . . .' No, thank you.

'Strange they knew so little about someone they cared so much for,' Evelyn said, clearly on a fishing expedition.

Phillip shrugged.

'Yet they had her bank account details,' she continued. Evelyn was sure that was somehow the key to Dee's disappearance.

Phillip nodded, his eyes fixed on the empty space where the car had been.

'I really love your train set,' Evelyn said. Perhaps a change of topic might bring him back out of his mind.

'Thanks for walking me home that morning,' Phillip said as he turned his gaze to her face. His eyes weren't quite brown. Or yellow. Or green. They were speckly, and Evelyn found herself mesmerised. If he had asked her to do a handstand she would have complied.

'You're welcome,' she said to fill the silence. Her face pinkened as she basked in his appreciation.

'I get lost sometimes.'

'Well, we all do,' she said as her hand reached out and patted his elbow. She willed her arm down to her side. It reluctantly stayed there as it awaited instruction. She and Phillip were still looking at each other.

'I have a box. A mind-box. Most of the time it's tucked under the bed, far away where I can't see it, but I always know it's there,' he said. Evelyn thought that was a bit like her errant arm. She couldn't feel it, but she knew it was hanging there vying for her attention. 'Every now and then I need to open it and see all the things I can't unsee,' he said. His eyes were still directed at her, but they looked at a faraway place. 'It has compartments, but they're in a different order each time I open it. Car accidents here, faces of distraught family members there. Faces contorted with loss. They're the most vivid. Every face, every eye, every wrinkle, every hand that rushes to the face or head. Whenever something terrible happens, people touch their face, try to hide it or hold their heads like they're trying to hold their brain in,' he said, his hands mimicking each reaction.

Evelyn had no idea what to say. Her arm was standing to attention, ready to plug in and suck some of the worry out of him. An industrial vacuum cleaner. Evelyn had spare sad space – no storage fee. Her breaths weakened and her eyes filled as she stood there brimming with feelings.

'Anyway,' he said as his eyes came back from wherever they'd been. 'I just wanted to thank you for walking me home when I was stuck.' He didn't have as much control over his arms as Evelyn did, and his hands reached over and clutched her shoulders. He gave them a little squeeze and said, 'You're a good person.'

'I would really like to come and play trains sometime,' she said before she could catch herself. She tried to avoid inviting herself to things for fear of looking desperate. The good person comment was pushed to the back recesses of her mind and instantly locked away ever so tightly, until she had the fortitude to deal with it.

'No time like the present,' Phillip said.

He gestured her inside and made her a cup of tea. She chose not to look inside the cup. Seeing something dirty was worse than knowing it to be. Phillip set the trains in motion and turned on the lights. The village was shrouded in moonlight from a lamp in the far corner, and they began putting all the villagers inside their houses for the night. Evelyn's face was brighter than the moon lamp.

'Some hay bales would look nice in those fields,' Evelyn said, pointing over at the hilly far corner that was too empty. Phillip got out some sticky tape and set out some strips in front of them, sticky side up. He gave Evelyn some scissors, some tattered brown flaky string and placed a small old bowl in front of her. A bowl with a flower necklace. Together they cut up the string into tiny flakes over the bowl, but it wasn't until he sprinkled the string flakes onto the sticky tape that Evelyn realised his vision. They sprinkled and rolled up their respective sticky tape pieces covered with string flake, and placed their hay bales on the rolling fields under the moon lamp.

'I'm going to a model train swap meet next Saturday, would you like to come?' Phillip asked.

Evelyn most certainly did.

CHAPTER TWELVE

It was Sunday, and Evelyn got out of bed feeling on top of the world. Don had phoned to ask whether she would like to see a film and Evelyn explained she was taking a neighbourhood boy to the zoo. The words 'Would you like to come along?' had fallen out before she had a chance to catch them. 'Sure would,' Don had said warmly. Christ. Don was to meet her at the laundromat at eight forty-five sharp, Ben was to be collected and then they should arrive at the zoo around opening time.

Evelyn had set her alarm for six, to give her plenty of time to make up a picnic basket. She chose the red tartan blanket for them to sit on, whistled as she made sandwiches and finished with ten minutes to spare. It wouldn't do to keep Don waiting.

The pair made small talk as Evelyn directed him to Ben's apartment block, and Evelyn flew out of the car to collect the boy. After ringing the doorbell, she practised her relaxed smile. The door opened suddenly, and Ben's mum was greeted with a startled half-formed happy face. June shook her head and muttered a 'for fuck's sake' as Ben pushed past her. He skidded at the top of the stairs, turned back and gave his mum a hug. Evelyn gave her a piece of paper with her phone number on it, in case she wanted to check in, and then she and Ben scooted down the stairs.

Ben stopped dead outside Don's car and asked Evelyn who the man inside the vehicle was. Evelyn could quite understand his reticence and explained that Don was actually a decent man, despite his appearance, and introduced them.

'But he's a stranger, Evie,' Ben said. His foot was half inside the car, and he willed himself to stop and examine his instincts.

'Well, you know my name,' Don said kindly, 'we're going to have a nice time and Evelyn is going to be right there with us the whole day.'

'Evie doesn't like to talk about nice days,' Ben said. 'She says it's a waste of time,' he added as he clamoured into the car. Don asked him what he meant as he put on his belt. 'Evie got a message the other day saying "Have a nice day" and it made her really mad because it was a waste of time,' Ben explained.

Evelyn went fire engine red, as that message had been from Don. She braved a look over at him, and saw he was grinning from ear to ear and looking at her endearingly.

She tried not to smile, but her face ignored all instructions and, before she knew it, she was laughing along with Don.

'What's funny?' Ben asked.

'Nothing. Sometimes people just laugh,' Don said, before talking about himself for a while. Ben seemed most interested in the fact Don was a paint specialist and he told Don all about the paintings he did in art class. Evelyn looked out the window and revelled in this sense of having a family. She'd never had one of her own and it was sweet background music.

When they got to the zoo, Don opened the boot and asked Ben to pick a ball. Evelyn thought this was a dreadful idea, as it would be cumbersome to carry a ball about, but Ben and Don examined them with such delight that she let them be. But she made it clear that she would not be the one carrying it around when they got sick of it. They grinned idiotically at her when she expressed her concerns, and she filed the 'I told you so' dance away for later.

While she waited in line, Ben and Don went to a patch of grass near the gates and kicked the soccer ball around. Ben listened to Don's coaching, as the boy had obviously had very little, and he only missed the ball three times out of five by the time Evelyn got to the front of the queue and called for them.

When the booth lady pushed the EFTPOS machine through the small semi-circle cut out of the perspex, Don flopped his card on it before Evelyn could reach over with hers. Aside from the fright, she was most annoyed that he did this without discussion. Don saw the annoyance on her face and proffered a smile and a small shrug. He was so annoying, yet she wasn't as irritated as she should be. Which rankled her even more. She added it to her list of gripes, right under Don forgetting to indicate earlier while driving.

Inside the gates, she opened out the map and called for a planning meeting. Ben just stood there, tapping his foot on the ground, itching to go.

'What's your favourite animal?' Don asked him.

'I don't even know,' Ben said. His face dropped.

Don put his hand on his shoulder and told him about the time he spent so long trying to decide which lollies he wanted that his mum just walked out of the shop, and he went crying after her with no lollies at all.

'It can all be a bit overwhelming sometimes,' Don said gently. When Ben asked him what that word meant, he said, 'It's when you're so full of feelings that you think you're going to explode.'

Evelyn thought this was sweet and became a little over-whelmed herself. She couldn't believe she hadn't mapped out a plan before they got there to avoid all of their feet being stuck in quicksand, and their minds all agog with options. Don suggested they start on the left and make their way around the outside until they got back to where they were. Evelyn said it just wasn't possible to do the whole thing properly in one day. Ben said he didn't care about doing it properly, but that he'd like to see something before the zoo closed.

They decided to follow Don's outer circle plan and set off. Ben ran on ahead and kept doubling back to make sure Evelyn and Don were still coming as they meandered up and down the wooden pathways through the monkeys. Evelyn didn't like monkeys much. They were often mean to each other, and the littlies seemed to enjoy irritating the grown-ups. Although she liked that the grown-ups didn't give them the time of day and held fast.

When they got to the hippos, Evelyn stood mesmerised. There was one that floated along in the water, his big eyes sitting up on top, taking them all in. He obviously thought he was at the zoo looking at them and Evelyn appreciated the juxtaposition, although she didn't say so. The otters were lovely too; busy little creatures weaving their way around all the rocks with speed. She wasn't sure what their purpose was, but she appreciated that they had one.

When they sat on the grass and spread out their picnic for lunch, Evelyn kicked off her sturdy boots. She was momentarily horrified to see her toes were wet with sweat, but she decided not to care. They devoured their sandwiches and Ben said thank you without prompting. Bits of sandwich flew out of his mouth every which way as he spoke, but Evelyn chose not to care about that either.

Over the way, a woman atop a path let her pram go for the smallest of seconds. The pram began rolling down the path and Don got up off the blocks like an Olympic runner, sped over and slid along the grass. His foot stopped the pram halfway down the hill, and he got up gracefully and pushed the pram back to the mother as he grinned and waved over at Evelyn and Ben. Evelyn waved back.

'Someone you know?' Don asked.

She started as she realised he was sitting right there. The pram incident had never happened, and she told herself to be more careful with her faraway mind while she was out in public.

'Were you off with the fairies, Evie?' Ben asked. 'My mum says I'm always off with the fairies.'

'Sure was, Ben,' Evie said. Her mother had always said that to her too, and she looked at him with sadness. Maybe he was consigned to a life of dreams as well. Evelyn stood up and shook herself. The others followed suit, but they were only shaking off crumbs.

The rest of their expedition – with the exception of the seals, who could have entertained Evelyn for hours – was all a blur. Although she did enjoy Don's animal facts much more than she let on. Apparently, elephant herds were made up of females and the only males in the herd were young calves, who leave home at fifteen to go and live by themselves. The head female was called a matriarch.

'Much like our Evelyn here, hey Ben?' Don said, smiling that stupid goofy smile that was starting to grate on Evelyn's nerves. Clearly her little herd today needed a matriarch, given how juvenile they were – running about making animal noises at the top of their voices. She couldn't stop the smile when she saw how happy Ben was, though, which she hoped didn't give Don the impression she was supportive of his antics.

Evelyn shouldn't have been surprised when Don told Ben that elephants were vegetarians. They were always swirling greenery up into their little mouths with coiled trunks. But when she found out they spent up to eighteen hours a day eating, she nearly fell over. Such big creatures. Evelyn wondered why they didn't just sit on some fat slow pigs and make pork patties. Surely that would save them some eating time. And they drank a bathtub of water a day by sucking it halfway up their trunk and squirting it into their mouths. They were not efficient animals, that's for sure – they had to work so hard to just live.

Evelyn was none too keen to go to the Australian animal section, but she enjoyed finding out that kangaroos alternate their legs when swimming. Next time Ben came in on Tuesdays with questions, she decided it would be a lot easier to cheat and ring Don. Perhaps she should ask him to explain how planes stayed in the air, but she didn't want to encourage him. And so Evelyn, as much as she tried not to enjoy herself, found herself caught up in all sorts of wonder. A couple of times she found a bench to sit on while Ben and Don kicked the ball around, but she mostly participated in their day.

By the time they got back to Ben's, Evelyn was spent. She handed him the leftover sandwiches, for just in case, and walked up the stairs to return him. When they got there,

Ben's mum opened the door. Ben showed her the soccer ball Don had given him and raced through into his room.

'Who the fuck is Don?' June asked as she bristled.

'He works in the paint section at the hardware store, and he helped me paint my wall blue,' Evelyn said, thinking this explanation would suffice.

'I wouldn't have let Ben go if I'd known there was a man going,' June said. After stepping out into the foyer and pulling the door closed behind her, she stood uncomfortably close to Evelyn. Again. Evelyn noticed that the young woman had green eyes. The murderous look in them didn't escape her either. June was fully squared up and ready to attack – backed by all her demons and frustrations at the world at large. Evelyn stepped forward into the remaining few millimetres of space between them. Their toes touched and neither of them moved.

'Well, he's a lovely man and I don't really give a fuck what you think,' Evelyn said as she reached her limit. 'You do what you have to do. Pack up your child, never bring him into the laundromat again, I don't give a shit.' Evelyn leaned forward into June's space. 'Ben is a lovely kid, I didn't mean any harm and he had the time of his life.' A bit of spit came out on her 'f' and landed on June's face. Neither said anything about it. 'I'll see you on Tuesday . . . or I won't. But whatever the fuck has made you so sad and miserable needs to be dealt with. You're not the only suffering human on the planet,' she said, stabbing June in the chest three times with her finger.

Ben's mum released a big smile. It was so unexpected to both of them that Evelyn smiled too. June let out a squeak of a giggle and Evelyn let out a big breath that turned into a guffaw. Neither of them had laughed so freely for so long, and they looked a maniacal mismatched pair standing on the landing. Ben opened the door and peeked through like he was checking the dark for monsters. He went straight over and stood between them and wrapped a thin arm around each of their thighs.

'Well, this is an almighty group hug, isn't it?' Evelyn said as the hug became hot metal and she had to let go. For a microsecond she had fallen into it, but she willed herself away.

There's fragile and there's brittle. For that moment, Evelyn wasn't made from blood and guts and bones. She was a pile of paper-thin autumn leaves waiting to be kicked about, rustling at each feeling. This hug had kicked her precarious pile of leaves and she tried to pull away before she shattered into a million pieces.

'Pull yourself together,' she silently told herself in anger. The others stood back and looked at her. Although they couldn't see it, Evelyn felt her arms flailing around, trying to catch all the pieces of herself, like one of those contestants in a wind tube trying to catch as much money as they could before the buzzer went off.

'Ooof, don't mind me young man, I had a moment,' Evelyn said by way of explanation.

'What's a moment?' Ben asked.

'Sometimes grown-ups have a burst of feelings that explode in their chests, and they have to wait a minute while everything settles,' Evelyn said kindly.

'Like when the boys at school say no one likes me. That makes my feelings explode,' he said flippantly. The two women froze for a moment, then Evelyn said she had to go. Her insides had returned and were now safely tucked inside a thickening enamel shell.

'Perhaps you can have a think about another place you'd like to go,' she said to Ben, but her eyes were on his mum. Strategy. It's harder to say no in front of the kid. She got a shrug in response from the mother and a shudder of excitement from the boy, who was also gauging his mother for a reaction. He, like Evelyn, took the shrug as a yes and they smiled at each other conspiratorially for the briefest of seconds. They knew to leave it at that.

'Bye, Evie,' Ben called out as she walked down the stairs.

'Tuesday,' Evelyn called out over her shoulder.

'I can walk from here,' she said, with not a skerrick of grace, when she got back to Don.

'Have a nice evening,' he said good-naturedly and winked at her. She smiled a brief, real smile and headed off across the park. When she got home, she sat in the bath with the shower running as hot as she could stand. She pulled up her knees until they were tucked up under her chin, hugged her shins and pushed her eyebrow bones into her kneecaps while she unashamedly cried out loud, throwing in a guttural moan from time to time. Part of her wished she'd asked Don back for a drink, but most of her didn't. She just didn't know when she had become who she was.

CHAPTER THIRTEEN

*E*velyn was surprised to hear her phone ringing, especially when she saw June's number displayed. She didn't like night phone calls, and quickly steeled herself.

'Evie,' Ben said quietly. Whispers can be loud, Evelyn thought, and decided he must be in a quandary.

'What's up, Ben?' she asked casually. She had become instantly alert, shuffled to a sitting position on the side of her bed and found herself in a terrible case of the dizzies. Was she having a heart attack? An actual heart attack? The nausea abated and the vague snowflakes trickling down the brown background in front of her eyes faded slowly. The room morphed into her vision, and she almost missed being blind.

'Mum's on the floor in the kitchen,' he said, sounding puffed.

'Does it look like she fell over?' Evelyn asked. She wasn't experienced in actual emergencies, but she had been the hero in so many imaginary ones that she had a lot to draw on.

They had been so real that her body and mind had felt the trauma as she worked through them, so the butterflies and rising panic were not unfamiliar. Besides, this was exactly why she followed people home. So she'd know where to go in an actual emergency.

'No, she's crawling around the floor counting the ants.'

This was a most unexpected development.

'Go to your room, but don't hang up the phone. I'm coming, Ben.' Evelyn reached under the bed and pulled out some shoes.

'Okay,' he said, 'I'm in my room, now.' A quiet whisper. Good. 'What if Mum notices her phone is missing?' Crescendo.

Evelyn's shoes were on, and she stood up without rushing. She didn't want to get dizzy again. The last thing the boy needed was for her to faint.

'She's busy counting ants,' Evelyn said. Nothing like injecting a bit of logic into the situation. She realised she'd put her shoes on before her pants and cursed herself internally. These were precious seconds. She sifted through her drawers and found a pair of casual hippy pants she wore around the house in summer. They had flared legs and she wrangled herself into them despite having shoes on. She patted her breasts and decided to spend a few moments putting on a bra; she needed to be at her best. 'I'll be there in seven minutes or so. I know it seems like a long time, but it's not. Can you hear anything?'

'No. Do you think she's all right?' he asked, desperation creeping into his voice.

'She's going to be fine. Sometimes grown-ups just need to have a crawl on the floor, Ben. Sometimes the world gets too much for them too. Like when the kids at school pretend you don't exist and you want to crawl up into a ball in the corner.' Evelyn spoke calmly, slowly. She grabbed her keys from the key bowl; thank God they were there.

It's not like she hadn't tried designated key spots before, but they had always failed, until recently when she had stumbled across a small stained-glass bowl. As soon as she had seen it, she knew she would feel the same joy every time she saw it, no matter how many times that would be. The red, orange and yellow glass panes reflected light like a disco ball, and sometimes she watched the light shapes dance around just for fun, although it wasn't without the odd pang of guilt. The bowl had been part of a nearby café's ambience, and Evelyn had put it in her pocket while nobody was looking. She was not a natural, nor regular, thief but she just had to have that bowl. Each time she went to the café now, her tips got bigger and bigger to make up for it. She'd probably paid for the bowl at least three times now.

'I'm out the door and walking down the street. You know the fish and chip shop?' she asked Ben. Distraction time.

'Yes.'

'And can you picture the end of the street, just before I turn in to the park?' Evelyn realised she had two different shoes on, both left ones. Her right foot was struggling, so she overcompensated. She must look like Quasimodo, if Quasimodo limped. Her mind wandered to the sack race when she was Ben's age. A shuffle forward with one foot, a loop around movement with the other to bring the sack back around . . .

'I'm in the park and I can see where Don parked the car when we went to the zoo. Do you remember how you nearly didn't get in the car?' she asked.

'Yes.' Nothing more.

She told him how clever his reaction was that day and how mature his thought processes were, just like calling her tonight. 'I'm really glad you called me, Ben, I'm going to help you.' She stopped at a tree across the road and put her head against it. The bark was papery, and she pulled off thin strips as she garnered her strength and pushed the pain of her right foot into the far distance before crossing the road and standing at the entrance door. This time it was not held open by a rock.

'Okay, love. I'm going to need you to walk to the front door and buzz me in, do you think you can do that quietly?'

'Yes.'

Evelyn waited for minutes. Probably only two of them, which she used to ponder. Minutes were long, but when they were strung together they lost their value. When she raced about, Evelyn's minutes became seconds and when she waited, they became interminable. When she sat in the middle between racing and waiting, she felt like they were flitting by without purpose. She often found herself speeding up to the point she needed to have little sits, and she decided then and there to improve her relationship with minutes. God knows, they weren't going to alter their behaviour to suit her. She'd start now, she thought, and focused on a succulent plant just to the right of the door, underneath the natives. An accidental succulent. A wayward fall of a leaf that sat on its side and just was until it eventually took root and off it went. 'That's a plant who knew how to use its minutes,' she thought to herself, when the front door buzzed. The noise was an offensive groan that gave her a fright, which she swallowed down in two gulps as she took to the stairs. Emanating residual fright wouldn't do Ben any good.

When she got to the main door, she whispered, 'It's me, Evelyn,' into the doorframe. Nothing. She tapped ever so lightly, and Ben cracked the door. The harsh light on the landing reflected off his wide-open eyes and Evelyn's heart melted. He looked frightened and relieved at the same time. He blinked a couple of times while Evelyn pushed the door ever so slightly. She pointed over Ben's shoulder towards his room, he nodded and set off. Evelyn followed, but not without a brief glance into the kitchen on her way through. Sure enough, June was on all fours in the far corner muttering to the floor. The spotted lino was her sole focus, giving Evelyn the confidence to straighten up as she walked. In Ben's room, she knelt on the floor and looked at Ben, now huddled at the head of his bed under the doona.

'I think she's sick,' he said, his eyes going side to side like he was trying to count railway carriages on a passing train. Thirty-six carriages in a few seconds.

'I think so too,' Evelyn said, 'but don't worry, she's going to be okay.' Assurance. Evelyn met Ben's teddy bear Vil. Three times she repeated Will, because why would anyone call a teddy Vil? In the end he said V for Victor and she understood. Instead of asking where the name Vil had come from, she snuggled the teddy into his shoulder and asked him to lie down. She told him that, one way or another, either herself or his mum would be right there in the morning, and that the day would be what days are – there no matter what. His eyes relaxed as she spoke and, as she tucked him in, she asked if he had a favourite picture book. Of course she knew he was big enough for chapter books, but sometimes, even if you're a grown-up, it's okay to return to a great picture book. One that brings back happy memories. She had noticed a stack of books on the bottom shelf of a blue bookcase when she entered the room. The other shelves proudly displayed trucks and figurines that had seen better days.

'Yes, *Wilfred Gordon McDonald Partridge*,' he said, jumping out of his cocoon and racing over to pick it up. 'It's about a boy with a long name who visits old people and realises they're cool.' He climbed back under the doona, into the warmth. 'Like me and you, Evie,' he said, holding out the book with two hands. Evie supposed she was old to a young boy, opened the cover and began reading it out loud.

There wasn't a lot of halfway in Evelyn's life at the best of times, and as soon as she started reading, she was the book. The old people's home came to life, and swirling exaggerated figures wandered around Ben's room espousing what memories were with watery eyes and saggy bodies. Yet there was an underlying pep in their steps. Ben became the boy gathering up his precious belongings and giving them to his favourite old lady – she sure did resemble Evelyn – who was reminded of moments past. Treasured moments. Evelyn fought back tears as she read, and Ben became torn between being mesmerised by the book and being enchanted by Evelyn, who was there yet somewhere else.

When the book finished, Evelyn transitioned, tucked it securely under Ben's pillow, patted his head and told him that everything was going to be fine. He believed her.

But when she went to stand, her left knee collapsed. Between her foot being cooped up in the wrong shoe and her kneeling on the floor for far too long, she could barely put one foot in front of the other. The poor lad had enough on his plate without her being incapacitated, so she hid her hurt by doubling over like Miss Nancy in the book and tucking her arms in T-rex style. That way she'd look like she was creeping rather than incapable. All this quick thinking made her realise that she was, in fact, quite good in a real-life crisis.

After she left Ben's room, she leant on the walls for two steps before lowering herself to the floor. Now that she didn't have to be strong for Ben, she found it prudent to crawl to the kitchen. When she reached the doorway and saw June in the opposite corner, she couldn't wipe the smile off her face. She gently coughed so as not to give the woman a fright. June looked up, startled, then looked back down hurriedly.

'Hello,' Evelyn said casually, 'I've done myself a mischief and my knee doesn't work. Looks like we're both on the floor for a while.' Amusement dominated her tone. June's face went from 'What the fuck are you doing here?' to 'I don't care what the fuck you're doing here' to 'Thank God you're here' in a millisecond. Evelyn was secretly pleased, but she kept her face neutral. Switzerland.

'I had a trip,' June said weakly. 'I'm fucked.'

Evelyn went to speak but all the words got stuck in her throat. A bottleneck of all the things she wanted to say and a myriad of things she didn't all backed up. The words were fighting their way to her mouth. Her brain was swatting away the wrong words, but they didn't go down far enough past the good words. They kept bobbing to the surface, pushing the right words further and further down. The wrong words were much better swimmers, so Evelyn threw the right words lifebuoys, but they just couldn't hold on tight enough, especially with the bad words pulling them down by the legs. Evelyn had strong words with herself, with her brain, with her throat, and slowly, slowly she willed the bad words down to her stomach, allowing the good words to rise to the top.

'It can happen to anyone, dear,' she finally said. She didn't even know those words were there, but she gave them a pat on the back. The amusement returned as she imagined a drone shot of them both crouched on all fours from above. Evelyn began to giggle and then laugh, June joined in.

'Everything's okay, Ben, go back to bed,' June said between gasps. Evelyn looked behind her and saw Ben, Vil flopped at his side.

'Everything's fine, Ben. Do what your mum said and head back to bed,' she said. It was important for the adults to have a united front. He smiled at Evelyn, who still had tears running down her face, then left.

Evelyn began to distract June from the ants and coax her out of the room. She told June to watch out for the pothole, to go around a log and to be careful of a protruding tree root. June focused and followed Evelyn's directions diligently. Much easier than ploughing through ants on a mission to take over the world one human at a time. Evelyn was glad for the distraction herself; it hadn't taken long for her to see ants in the lino flecks either – and she wasn't even tripping.

When June got to the doorway, both women crawled through the lounge room to June's bed. Evelyn gave June a boost, and on the third try, June finally made it to base camp. Evelyn straightened out her legs and massaged her wayward knee. She was going to have to get up before she did a hip.

June lay on the bed in a tight ball, eyes closed, moaning torturedly from time to time. Evelyn supposed she was in sleep limbo, flitting between the real world at its worst and badlands on the top of the faraway tree sleep.

Evelyn rolled over to all fours and eased herself upright. The next few days were going to be difficult, what with a sore knee, a bruised foot and the dilemma of a boy who deserved a responsible mother. She hobbled to the bathroom in search of a bandage. When she opened the drawers and cupboards, she was most impressed. It was well stocked and the items that should be together, were. A mother's bathroom. She found a clipped, neatly rolled bandage behind the betadine and band-aids, sat on the edge of the bath and wrapped her knee. While she was there, she saw a case similar to her lockpicking kit under the sink, although it wasn't genuine leather and the zipper was cheap. It caught twice as she opened it, and her chest contracted when she saw its contents. Three needles, a bag of powder and two cigarette filters – God knows what they were for. She placed it back where she'd found it, almost secreted behind a disused travel bag and a curling iron, and stood up. She took a few moments and found herself looking in the mirror.

It was a good thing she had caught a glimpse of herself. The look on her face just would not do. She slowly manipulated the anger, the rage, the fear, the sadness, the grief until they no longer showed. There was nothing she could do right then to address the goings-on, but she could check on Ben. Evelyn opened his door quietly and saw he was fast asleep with Vil tucked in under his chin. He was too old for a teddy, but she could see why he still grasped onto it. Everyone needs a friend. A friend who loves unconditionally, who doesn't judge, who listens, who evaporates fear with a single hug. Perhaps Evelyn wasn't too old for a teddy either.

Evelyn opened the linen cupboard and pulled out two blankets and a sleeping bag. She went to the lounge room, put the blankets on June and draped herself in the sleeping bag as she settled into the armchair. It's not like she wasn't going to wake up sore anyway. She hoped her sleep would be less fitful than June's. But she doubted it.

CHAPTER FOURTEEN

*E*velyn was bewildered, which was not her preferred state of being. She knew the solution lay with Don. He was stable. Reliable, which was a most underrated quality. But now wasn't the time for solutions. Now was about crafting a note for June and getting Ben to school. Ben was standing in the doorway looking at her.

'Good morning, young man,' Evelyn said, sitting forward in her chair. Her body had the weariness that comes with a long flight. As she made it to the edge of the armchair, she farted. This sent Ben into peals of laughter, which were exacerbated by him trying to laugh silently. His body shook like an earthquake and his breaths were spasmodic hot spring geysers. Evelyn joined in, despite her brain handing in a strong no permission slip. Each time it looked like their laughter was subsiding, a fresh round began, and Evelyn wondered whether survival was possible.

June woke up and looked at them, bleary-eyed. She joined in as far as a woman at the tail end of a bad trip could and asked what on earth was so funny in between her half giggles, half chokes. As it all subsided, Ben muttered, 'Evelyn farted when she tried to stand up,' and a new round began. Evelyn finally convinced her mind that farts shouldn't be that funny and managed to direct Ben to get his uniform on.

'Let's not worry about last night at the moment,' Evelyn said. June lay back down and put her hands over her face. 'I'm going to get Ben to school, and you can rest up.' Evelyn's knee let her know of its sorry existence and she forced her right foot into its left shoe. Turned out feet had a memory, and it told Evelyn that it was not at all happy about being put back into its shoe prison. Ben helped her stand up.

'You're a sweet boy,' Evelyn said, pushing down on his shoulder harder than she'd meant as she leveraged herself to a standing position. 'I was just saying to your mum how lovely it would be to have dinner at Don's tomorrow night.'

'Oh, can we, Mum? Can we?' Ben was unable to contain his excitement. June nodded weakly, which sent Ben off into a long series of questions, from whether Don would want to play soccer to what they would have for dinner to where does he even live. Evelyn shuffled him out the door and told him to wait a minute. She told a half-asleep June that she would be in the laundromat all day if she needed her. June rolled over in response. Evelyn shrugged. There was nothing worse than being embarrassed, she supposed, as she started down the stairs, leaning heavily on the banister.

Ben went on ahead through the park, kicking the soccer ball around. By the time they got to the bakery, Evelyn was spent. She organised their breakfast and lunch and sent Ben on his way. There was no way she'd make it to the school and back, and she went home to release her right foot and re-strap her knee before opening her stable-style door and putting on the best face she could for her customers.

That evening, when she closed the laundromat, relief flooded through her. Each minute of the day had pounded her and, despite feeling bruised, she headed straight to Don's house. She rapped on the door four short, sharp times. When he answered, he seemed surprised to see her. He had nothing on his feet, and a brief glance down showed he paid no attention to his toenails. At all. And the sparse tufts of hair on at least five of his toes were so offensive, she quickly moved her eyes up. Although she tried to ignore the rest of him as her eyes made her way up to his face, it was hard to avoid his thick calves, which would have made any Scottish dancer proud, his knobbly knees, and his groin, which was practically falling out of his too tight shorts. When she got to his face, he broke out in an easy asymmetrical smile. It was a pleasant relief from the rest of him, and she walked straight through the front door.

'How did you know where I live?' he asked. Although his question began quizzically, it became nonchalant so quickly, she knew the answer didn't matter.

'I just don't know where to start,' Evelyn said. He pointed straight down the hallway, and Evelyn gestured for him to go past, then limped along behind him. There was some sort of adrenaline dump coursing through her body, and she barely made it through the original kitchen and down the three steps to the backyard. He sat casually at a table that should have been thrown out years ago and watched her flop into a plastic chair that creaked as she sat. For a moment she was distracted by the fact that a plastic chair could even creak, then she launched into the tale of Ben's mum counting ants, of being debilitated by her right foot being cooped up in her left shoe, and kneeling for way too long in the old people's home full of swirling characters trying to define what memories were.

Don sat there listening, in no hurry to put the pieces into place. His goofy grin was giving her the shits, but she also saw the kindness underneath it. Surely by now he'd have some words of wisdom, so she paused. Nothing. So she continued and told him how she'd crawled to the kitchen and coaxed June out of the corner by pretending she had to avoid a variety of acts of God through an imaginary forest, and how she then boosted June up to the bed of stability. She mentioned that June and Ben were coming around to dinner the following night, so they could figure out this whole mess together.

'It's important to have backup plans, Don,' she said as she placed a printout in front of him. He looked down, clocked the foster care pamphlet, then said he was about to put on the barbeque. Perhaps she would like him to put on an extra chop or two? He was finding the whole situation a little amusing for her taste, but she was hungry.

Don went and got a bottle of wine, and thankfully returned in a shirt. Even if it was a sorry one. He handed her a quite lovely cut crystal wineglass and Evelyn relaxed back into her creaky plastic chair. She took at least three breaths; counted to five on the way in, held for three (she was going for five) and counted to five in her head as she let her breath out. She rinsed and repeated before asking Don what the old breathing technique was. She knew there was a number for each part of the breath cycle to create calm and wellness within oneself but was peeved that she couldn't remember the correct amount. Don said that perhaps any old number would do, and Evelyn went through another cycle of incorrect breathing counts just to recover from his ignorance.

Evelyn had to admit that food and a glass of wine was just what the doctor would order, and actually smiled at him. She felt so comfortable that she even picked up the chop with her fingers and just chowed down on it, sucking the bone at the end. She'd put the requisite amount of salad on her plate without being rude and ran her tongue around her teeth afterwards, to make sure she caught any errant leaves on her teeth while she wondered what sort of teeth elephants had, and how the hell they picked all the leaves out of them during their eighteen hours a day of eating vegetation. They must eat eighteen hours a day for the sole purpose of not having to address the salad film stuck steadfastly to their teeth, she concluded.

'Do elephants sleep standing up?' she asked Don.

'Mostly,' he said, without any apparent thought as to why she'd asked the question. This cemented, to Evelyn, why he was indeed the person to help her through the June–Ben crisis. Not once did Don ever appear to wonder why she needed to know things. He just accepted her for who she was.

'They sleep more lying down when in captivity.' His fact-stating was laced with sadness, which accentuated the accuracy of her conclusion.

'This is why I'm here, Don,' Evelyn said with so much affection she nearly choked on her teeth-cleaning wine sip. There was no need to finish her thought.

'Did you know I play the banjo?' he asked.

It was such an appropriate response that Evelyn nearly fell off her creaky plastic chair.

CHAPTER FIFTEEN

*E*velyn was nervous about the impending dinner. She had been debating what approach to take as she ironed and washed the day away. When she had decided some time ago that a laundromat was tailor made for her, the reasons were firmly based in the spaces she went to while performing domestic duties. It was cathartic, beneficial to her wellbeing and it created mind space for her to catch all her flying thoughts and put them in some sort of order. The downside was that it created space for her to catch all her flying thoughts and put them in some sort of order. The sheer scale of her duties had led to a severe case of overthinking.

Evelyn took a trip to her drawer of things past, in search of the card game she had kept since she was a child. Comic Families had created so many moments for Little Evelyn, and she thought the group tonight may need an ice-breaker after having dinner sprung on them. And just because she'd organised it did not mean it hadn't sprung up on her too. Being privy to June's dark-side proclivities had given Evelyn an unspoken power, and she had knowingly wielded it to get June to submit to the dinner. But the manoeuvre had been cheeky at best and manipulative at worst. Evelyn was not proud of herself, but her intention was to set the little family back on track. When she'd voiced this to Don, he had understood her intentions, but added that just because someone didn't mean to murder someone, did not mean that there wasn't a dead body. Sure, she had flicked some eye icicles at him, but she had kept her words firmly tucked away out of sight.

As she went through her drawer of things past, she happened across a photo of herself when she was in her late teens. Each time she looked at it, she reeled at how gaunt, underweight and unfocused she had been. She took a moment to revel in how far she had come. She hadn't always been such a helpful community member, a small business owner or able to sit on so high a horse. One day, teenage Evelyn had looked around at her friends (whose minds were in varying states of disrepair) and simply stood up, left, and travelled interstate with nothing but the clothes on her back. As she looked into her younger eyes, she decided it was time to be magnanimous with June. Although, with a child involved, it would be a very short rope.

Besides, if it all went to hell, she had a backup plan. Don hadn't paid much attention to the foster care pamphlet she had left on his back table. But he had seen it. Evelyn didn't mind that he hadn't spoken about it. Some people take longer to absorb things than others. She placed the photograph back in the drawer. It was yellowed and beginning to fade, so she wrapped it in the thin golden silk scarf with the Klimt painting on it that had been given to her back when she could love. She placed the Comic Families card game into her pocket and headed to Don's.

When Evelyn arrived, an appropriate ten minutes early, she could hear Ben whooping through the open front door. This threw her temporarily, as she didn't expect June to be remotely punctual. She much preferred others gathering around her rather than joining an existing group.

'Helllllooooo,' Evelyn called out in her most cheery tone as she walked straight out the back towards Ben's laugh. He and Don were kicking the ball around, and June had made herself quite at home, sitting at the table that should have been thrown out years ago. Her feet were up on another chair, but she pulled them off when she followed Evelyn's disapproving gaze at her toes. Ben ran over and took Evelyn's hand.

'Come see the goalposts Don made, Evie,' he said as he pulled her across the grass. Don had made some makeshift goals out of broomsticks wrapped hurriedly in tinfoil. Even though they looked ludicrous, she complimented the shiny sticks.

'I'm helping Don with the pizzas,' Ben said with excitement and purpose.

'I have dip,' Evelyn said, putting her shopping bag down on the outside table. June said she would go and prepare a platter, as she had brought some cheeses and crackers. Don escorted her inside to show her where everything was, leaving Evelyn and Ben alone. Evelyn pulled out the card game and placed it in front of him. He did what any kid would do and began to look through the cards.

'These look really old,' he said. Evelyn said they were as old as Einstein and then fumbled when Ben asked how old Einstein was.

'Don't worry, Evie, Don will know,' he said as he continued looking at the pictures. Evelyn explained that there was a ma, pa, sister and brother in each family, and that each player had to build complete families by asking the other players for specific cards.

'They have very big heads and very little bodies,' he said, holding up two Fish-os and a Tater. 'Look, the Fish-o family are all fishing, and the Snips family are all hair cutters,' he said.

Evelyn chose not to say that it was all rather logical; the lad seemed to think he was espousing fascinating insights. God knows his ego must be bruised enough already.

'Look, Pa Drugs looks like Don,' he said, showing the card as Don and June arrived back at the table.

'Yes, that's the chemist family,' Evelyn said as she scrambled to fill the momentary awkwardness that had stopped the other two dead in their tracks, platters midair, at the word 'drugs'. Of all the families in all the world, Don had to look like Pa Drugs. She followed up with a brief explanation of her sentimental old-fashioned cards.

'Where are these from?' Ben asked. Evelyn explained that they were her dad's when he was little and that she kept them in her drawer of things past. A drawer full of things that reminded her of who she was.

'Oh, a memory drawer,' he said with glee. 'I keep my truck that my dad gave me and a picture of my nanna who died on my shelf. I'm going to put them in a drawer and have a memory drawer too, Evie.' He grabbed a couple of crackers, dipped them into the beetroot dip and plonked them into his mouth whole. His teeth went burgundy, and they were covered in cracker bits as he waffled away about all things sentimental.

Evelyn asked June what she would put in her drawer of things past. It was as good a way of getting to know someone as any.

'I don't keep the past,' she said, looking around for potential exits. Don suggested they play the ancient card game, and Evelyn thought he'd make a lovely international peacekeeper. It turned out they were all quite competitive and Ben beamed when he got the full Copper family and placed them down on the table.

'I wish I could draw like that,' Ben said as he marvelled at every card. 'Mum's really good at drawing.' Evelyn came third to Ben and June, even though she had tried to win.

She dry swallowed three times to keep her inner sore loser from bubbling to her face.

Don and Ben had put together quite the array of pizzas. There was pulled lamb and fetta, a salami and bocconcini cheese, and a fancy margherita in case of vegetarianism. Don thought he'd try to cover all bases, no pun intended. June said she loved dad jokes, Evelyn said she didn't and they ate quietly, except for Ben who regaled them with fun facts from *The Guinness Book of Records*. Who knew you could fit three and a half thousand toothpicks in a beard or that you could even do chin-ups with your little fingers.

As the eating wrapped up, Don explained that young Ben had told him he liked art. When the table had been cleared, a team effort, he set out a variety of paint tubes, different-sized brushes and four oblongs of thick cardboard, each larger than the painting paper he set down on each one. 'Maaaaaax,' Don said loudly before clicking his tongue over and over. Evelyn wanted to pull it out and shove it in his ear. A white cat with a weak jaw, a half-closed eye and brown shoes came over. Don held it up and said that everyone was to paint a portrait of Max. Evelyn didn't like following orders, but this battle was let through to the keeper when she saw how enthusiastically June and Ben embraced the activity.

When Ben said there was no brown, June leaned over and plopped some red, blue and white on his card and suggested he mix it all up. It was tender and Evelyn was glad she was sitting down. When she looked down at her blank piece of paper, she nearly vomited. She felt self-conscious, exposed. Her insides were on the outside. She looked over and saw June painting two swirls of fairy floss. Clearly the woman had talent, which added to Evelyn's discomfort.

'What has that got to do with the cat?' Evelyn asked, and a little triumph snuck its way into her tone.

'You'll see,' June said with a big fat smile. It was radiant and contagious.

When she looked over to see Don's progress, she saw a psychedelic sky. He was drawing a cat on a separate piece of paper and cutting out its facial features to make a stencil. Ben had finished a long brown fence and a sun in the sky.

Evelyn forced her displacement down to the bottom of her boots, filled her brush with blue and jabbed away. A textural sky formed, and she added a small faraway air balloon in tribute to her and Don's imaginary balloon journeys. She flopped out a large soft serve of white on her card and did her best to keep the enjoyment off her face.

'How do I do clouds?' she asked no one in particular. June came over and put her hand over Evelyn's, and together they jabbed away like woodpeckers. She filled her sky with blustering clouds in a thirty-knot westerly, and a mini piece of uptight left her body with each stroke.

Before long, Ben held up a cottonwool almost-cat atop a fence, June held up a sultry reclined feline with a smirk in its eyes and large pink headphones over its ears. Don held up a lion cat skulking through a graffitied alleyway under a fantastical sky, and Evelyn proudly held up her cloud-filled sky. The front and centre cloud morphed into a cat face if you looked closely with your head tilted and one eye shut.

Don and Ben went off to get the lamingtons.

'Thanks for the other night,' June said to Evelyn, almost looking her in the eyes. Evelyn nodded curtly, but her eyes were soft. No offending behaviours would be addressed tonight.

CHAPTER SIXTEEN

*E*velyn had been so distracted with June and Ben, that she had forgotten all about the missing girl. When she shut up shop later in the week, she hobbled up the stairs, collected her leather case with the fat gold zip from her drawer of things past and limped across the park to the missing girl's flat. The outer door to the apartment block was shut, so Evelyn plastered her best 'Oh dear, I forgot my keys' face on and waited. Eventually, a man returning from work held the door open for her and she made her way to the second floor. Although she was slowed by her throbbing knee, she walked along with confidence. A person with purpose is a person who belongs, she chanted internally until she got to the girl's door.

Evelyn slid out her kit and raked the pins. It clicked open first time. The glass balcony doors faced her as she walked down the short hallway. It was still light enough to see out, but she could see a vague reflection of herself in the glass. It was complete, yet faded and opaque, and she looked like a ghost, if ghosts were real. Evelyn pulled the thick curtains across the windows for privacy, then turned her attention to the room. It was empty, except for the dust tumbleweeds and bits of rubbish scattered across the carpet. She went into the kitchen, which was empty also. Nothing in the drawers or cupboards except a discarded broken potato peeler. The bathroom was empty except for some used cottonwool balls on the basin bench and an empty Panadol sleeve in the cupboard behind the mirror.

Evelyn went to the bedroom next. There was an upended drawer on the floor, and when she opened the doors to the built-in wardrobe, she saw the large floral tin described by the serious helmet-haired lady. It was sitting on top of the hip-height drawers. The lid of the tin was loose, so Evelyn looked inside. There was a bank deposit book, with the last date on the stubs being more than six months ago, and some folded paperwork with a list of the league's members and their details. Under that was a solitary facedown five-cent piece. Evelyn checked the rest of the cupboards and found a duffle coat with a missing toggle, nothing in the pockets, and a pair of shoes with a broken heel. Evelyn left the flat with the tin and headed downstairs to report in to Phillip.

When Molly had told the policeman that she had the missing girl's bank account details, Evelyn's hackles had risen. And her instincts had clearly been on point. The girl had taken off with the league's money. Evelyn wondered about the effort of such a long ruse versus the payoff. It seemed incongruous.

When Phillip opened his door, he was pleased to see her and ushered her inside. He pulled out a stool from under the train set, sat her down and went to get them a cup of tea. It reminded Evelyn of when she was little and wasn't allowed to talk to her parents unless she could see them, which eliminated raised voices across rooms. Her mother had not obeyed the rule herself, however, and Little Evelyn ran across the house as quick as she could when called. The longer she took, the worse her mother's temper.

'Are you still coming on Saturday?' Phillip asked when he pulled out the other stool and sat beside her.

'Oh yes,' she said immediately, although it took her a moment to remember the upcoming model train fair. Evelyn had many internal rules, one of which was to reassess her life when she got so busy that she needed to write things down. It was a sign of things spiralling out of control, of being spread too thin, of losing equilibrium. She took a few deep breaths and sipped at her tea. Phillip didn't say anything more, and Evelyn appreciated the moment so she could pull herself together. It had been a big few days, and the tide was still in.

After the train had done two more laps, Evelyn told Phillip that she had searched the missing girl's apartment. And that she believed the girl had vanished on purpose. She had no idea why the girl would have infiltrated these women's lives and left with so little, given how long she had taken to befriend them, as she would have earned more by having an actual job for all those months.

Evelyn tasted frustration as she spoke. Phillip was listening, but he didn't say anything. She didn't want an ear, she wanted answers. Still, the answers, if he had any, would probably just grate on her nerves anyway. When she was upset, answers and solutions wound her up just as much as silent listening did – even if answers were what she thought she wanted.

As she slumped in the chair, her stomach folded over itself and she felt plumper than she was. When she was in the wars, she always felt like there were big red flashing hands and neon arrows all pointing towards her belly, just to make sure no one missed it. And she was certainly in the wars. She waded through her mind mud and found the string she needed to pull herself out. She was sulking, and she needed to tell herself so. That was the only way out.

There was work to be done. She had to take the tin to the girls – it was practice night at the pub – and explain that their friend wasn't missing at all; she had done a runner. Evelyn hadn't been on this side of a runner before, and she wondered whether anyone had ever looked for her, worried for her or cried for her when she had left and begun a new life. Perhaps. Perhaps not.

Evelyn told Phillip she was off to tell the girls about the empty flat, and to return the tin to the helmet-haired lady who had seemed so attached to it. At least there would be some good news.

'Things aren't always as they seem, Evelyn,' Phillip said kindly. She rankled when he suggested she listen rather than act; to let things take their own course because answers only bob up when there is space. 'Be open minded and try not to jump to conclusions.'

Evelyn made a conscious choice to let his words fly past, rather than let them in. After all, she was the most open-minded person she knew. Mostly. And she had a stellar set of listening ears, thank you very much. Mostly.

When she stood up this time, she knocked her bad knee on a table leg. Right on the funny bone. The pain soared through her whole body for an unpleasant moment before her knee vacuumed up the pain and made a throbbing ball right behind her kneecap. After she had recovered, mostly, she suggested to Phillip that he get himself a couple of pool noodles. He could slice them in half longways and tape them to the table legs to prevent other such injuries. He nodded thoughtfully with a smile in his eyes, and she left with the large round old cake tin curled in her arm.

CHAPTER SEVENTEEN

*E*velyn stood outside The Station Hotel and looked through the window. The practice games were underway, and she devised her entry plan. It would be best to wander in and sit out of the way and wait for a break in play. This would give her a chance to have a drink and come up with a sensitive way to tell the girls their friend had gone.

She sat closer to the bar than the pool tables and put the large old cake tin on the chair next to her. It had a faded red lid with a rooster etching on the top, and the base was covered in interlaced roses that had faded to a dull pink around the edges. She pictured the serious helmet-haired lady as a young girl, who would have been teased about her googly eyes in her thick glasses. Perhaps going to her grandma's, a sweet doubled-over lady with a big smile, and eating cake was the highlight of her week.

Andy looked over and saw Evelyn. When she started to rush over, Evelyn flicked her hand at the pool table to indicate she was in no hurry and to prioritise their sport, but Andy headed straight over anyway. Molly was hot on her heels.

'I have bad news, I'm afraid,' Evelyn said with a sympathetic nod. She had practised her 'I'm sorry' face when she was outside looking in.

'What, what?' Andy said with chopping hands. Evelyn picked up the tin and placed it on the table between them.

'She's not missing, she's just gone,' Evelyn said with her best 'there, there' face. She suddenly realised that it wasn't going to be as simple as that.

'How do you know? Where did you get the tin? What happened? But she's our friend?' Andy said. None of her questions were designed to be answered and her voice was higher and quicker than usual. Molly just sat there with a bowed head that she shook over and over again.

Evelyn explained that she had gone to Dee's apartment and found a spare key under the front door mat.

'There is no front mat,' Andy said, suddenly suspicious.

'Oh,' Evelyn said, her mind whirred and tried to find another lie. There wasn't one. She explained that she had broken in to look for clues and that the place was empty except for a potato peeler, a duffle coat with a broken toggle and a pair of shoes with a broken heel. The serious helmet-haired lady had spotted the tin and strode over to join them. Evelyn found the way she held her pool cue menacing.

Her faced hardened even more when she heard about the deliberate disappearance, then became resigned as she sat down. She signalled the rest of the team over and told the tall bored woman to cancel the rest of the practice session. When the opposing captain came over, the helmet-haired woman told her that everything was fine and to let them be, please. Evelyn wondered why she would say everything was fine when it wasn't, but it didn't take long to figure it out.

'Fucking cunt,' the helmet-haired woman said as she banged her fist on the table. Then she put her head in her hands. 'Why would she do this to us?' she added so quietly Evelyn could barely hear her.

'She was our friend. Was our friendship even real?' Molly asked, briefly looking up at Andy with tears in her eyes and betrayal on her face.

'I feel so stupid,' Andy said to no one in particular. They were all having their own moments. The pointy thin lady's eyes were darting around without focus, the woman with the bright clothes and the Tigger curls hugged herself so tightly Evelyn was worried she couldn't breathe, Molly continued to shake her head and Andy's face flicked between anger and sadness. The tall bored woman sat on the edge of the group. Her foot was at the angle where the nerve that shakes the whole leg was activated. Evelyn wanted to tell her to stop, but she remained still. It seemed the appropriate thing to do.

Just as Phillip predicted, all their stories began pouring out of their bellies and Evelyn saw the depth of the deception.

Dee had infiltrated the team, befriended them and grifted as many women throughout the whole league as she could. The pool league's coffers were just the icing; Dee had taken their own money too. The group went back to the beginning in an effort to find the moment. The moment they should have realised the truth. They were searching for answers that Evelyn knew they wouldn't find.

Dee was always professionally and expensively dressed and had told them she wanted to join the team so she had an outlet from her career. To have some meaningful relationships outside of finance, numbers and investments. And they had welcomed her with open arms. Dee always spoke of shares and bragged about the returns she was getting her clients. It was like a foreign language. Between the ups and downs of iron ore, oil, the booming ethical investment sector, and acronyms no one understood, it had all been a blur. Molly and Andy, who Dee had sidled up to from the beginning, had been the first to invest. Between them they scrounged seven thousand dollars and handed it over willingly. Within a couple of months, Dee's prediction of rising iron ore prices had come true and they were given back just shy of ten thousand dollars.

The girls had shouted drinks that night. Word spread throughout the league, seventy members in total, and they lined up to give Dee money. Some were given dividend payments while their principle remained invested, which furthered the investment influx. There had been agreement notes listing amounts received, the financial securities to be traded, dates when capital or profits could be requested – all of which added to the scam's legitimacy. No one had given much, but collectively it was a tidy sum. An amount that more than justified the long ruse. Evelyn had given up trying to add it up and just sat there and listened. Not because Phillip had told her to, but because she was speechless.

It wasn't the loss of money that upset Evelyn. After all, there was a part of her that wanted to say there are no shortcuts in life; that they somehow deserved what they got. But the more it went on, the more empathetic Evelyn became. She realised that trashy grabs like 'Woman Deceived by Love Rat' or 'Pensioner Loses Everything to Overseas Scam' were more than sensational headlines. There were real people behind the story. People don't have to be stupid to have bad things happen to them, sometimes bad people just happened to them. It made her feel guilty. She had prided herself on not judging others, yet here she was.

It was more than money though. Each unique loss was swirling through her skull. The helmet-haired lady had invested the money she was going to use to buy a motor scooter for her nan, and she also planned to replace her nan's front step with a ramp and put shower rails in. Now it was all gone. They spoke of a short lady who wouldn't be able to get pedal lifts on her car pedals now; another who handed over everything she had saved to get closer to her house deposit, no one in her family had ever owned their own home; someone who had sourced a car through Dee, it was probably stolen or a lemon; and the list went on. All of them handing Dee money in the hope of easing their lives, rather than out of greed.

'How are we going to tell them?' the lady with the Tigger curls asked. They all became still.

'This is all your fault,' the helmet-haired lady said to Andy and Molly, flicking her pointer finger between the two. It had been said with venom. They had been the only ones to make a profit.

'It's not anyone's fault,' Evelyn said calmly with upturned palms. Her comment was lost as the others turned on the two girls.

'They were probably in on it,' the bored tall lady said, coming to life.

'We were not,' Andy said desperately.

'We bought Sally with the money,' Molly said, throwing the keys at the helmet-haired lady. 'Take the car,' she added petulantly.

The helmet-haired lady said she didn't want their stupid old shitbox and threw the keys back. They hit Molly in the face, and she started to cry about more than her sore nose. Andy stood up, squared off to the helmet-haired lady and did 'Come on over here' hand gestures. Her face was thunder. The helmet-haired lady leapt to her feet and rose to the challenge.

'EVERYONE SIT DOWN NOW,' Evelyn said. Her voice was powered with a cocktail of feelings from June's bad trip, Ben who had to grow up before he should, Don's goofy grin and Dee, who had mowed through these women's lives and taken their money, their trust, and had left them full of embarrassment, doubt, guilt and shame. The group resumed positions and they looked a sad and sorry bunch.

'This is not their fault. The only person to blame here is Dee,' Evelyn said with authority. The group mumbled agreement. The helmet-haired lady said sorry; so did Andy. Evelyn suspected it wasn't Dee's first scam, and said so.

'It's time to go to the police,' she said as she sat up straight. She hadn't noticed she was as slumped as the rest of them. Andy said there was no point, the lady with Tigger curls said she just couldn't face the humiliation, the helmet-haired woman said they had to cancel the end of season celebration and trophy ceremony and the woman with the pointy chin said that was the least of their worries because they had to tell others who had invested that their money was gone. Evelyn said that if they couldn't muster the courage to go to the police about themselves, that they should think about the next group of vulnerable people that Dee was going to fleece because this was not one-off behaviour.

The brief almost-fight was soon forgotten and a bond now formed among the women. They united their shame, humiliation and embarrassment, then planned to speak to the other teams as a group. They collectively decided it was time to go to the police station.

'You'll come with us, won't you?' the helmet-haired woman asked Evelyn. There was a pleading in her tone that Evelyn couldn't refuse. As they walked down the road, Evelyn explained that they mustn't ding the bell when they got there and that they had to be patient. Other than that, the walk was eerily quiet as each person retreated into their own loss and shame.

Evelyn held the door open and ushered the group through. They all sat on the bolted down moulded plastic chairs to wait. No one could be bothered getting impatient and, before long, a thirty-something woman with a neat bun came out from behind the mirrored glass and ushered the group over. Evelyn stayed on her moulded plastic chair and watched. The constable had empathy in her eyes as Andy began their tale, and Evelyn was pleased to see them in good hands. She hoped the group wouldn't carry the betrayal forward when they met new people, and that they found trust and confidence again quickly.

Evelyn had always prided herself on doing just that when she went from one life to the next. Although, she suddenly realised, perhaps she carried everything forward. Perhaps she ran and ran with an ever-growing weight, becoming less and less able to love the further she went. A long addition sum sprang to mind: one life plus the next, carry forward infinity. June jumped into her head, and she wondered what she carried forward. Why she was barely able to tread water. The women at the counter didn't need her anymore, so she left without saying goodbye.

PART TWO

CHAPTER EIGHTEEN

*E*velyn was excited to be going to a swap meet, even
if it was a model train one. She admired people who
embraced their interests and created their own communities
with others, although she was surprised to see so many people
standing in line at the town hall. Phillip was at the top of
the stairs and, as she made a beeline for him, each person
she passed became displeased at her pushing in. She waved
and called his name the whole way, as did he, but the fact
that she was clearly joining someone didn't even dent the
annoyance of those in her wake. When she stood next to
him, her nose prickled. Her eyes followed the smell.

There was a man nearby in a coat that was shiny with
ingrained grime. His face was similarly grubby, and Evelyn
thought he looked like a chimney sweep from a different
century. When he smiled, she saw he sprouted a few stumpy
black teeth, and she put on her best neutral face.

The group of men around Phillip continued their talk of trains as though she hadn't even arrived, and Evelyn noted that she was relegated to the bottom of the social ladder along with smelly old mate standing on their periphery. Evelyn checked her watch and saw there was still an hour to go before the doors opened. She asked Phillip if he'd like a coffee. He shook his head but the two men next to him asked for cappuccinos, seeing she was going anyway. Now that they wanted something, they were prepared to introduce themselves. One was a tall birdlike man who scrunched his nose every few seconds. Evelyn wondered if it was a tic or whether he was unable to ignore the smelly elephant in the room. The other was a jolly ruddy-faced man who could have been anywhere between fifty and eighty. It was always hard to tell the ages of happy people. She did a doubletake at his pale blue overalls as she didn't believe anyone over ten should wear them unless they were working.

Evelyn headed off to the nearest coffee shop, and she soon found herself in a serious case of the sweats. Back when she was a schoolgirl, her sports teacher had told her off for saying 'sweating'. Apparently men sweat and women perspire. Evelyn wondered whatever happened to the harsh six-foot-five woman who had done her best to teach Evelyn how to catch a ball. The constant look of disgust on her face was what had sparked Evelyn to practise a variety of appropriate faces for her ever-growing set of social circumstances. It had held her in good stead over the years, proven just before when she had smiled warmly at the smelly man despite her disdain and sadness. Never mind that she still couldn't catch a ball.

Despite her obvious skills at adapting and settling into new groups, new social scenes made her nervous on the inside and sweat on the outside. But still she kept throwing herself out there in case the next group was going to be the one. Her one. This event was particularly challenging as the only conversation topic was trains, which she knew nothing about other than they created lovely new lands for her and her imaginary people to live in.

Evelyn returned with four coffees, handed one to the bird man, one to the chubby ruddy overalled cartoon man, and one to the smelly man before taking a large swig of her own.

'I didn't know if you had sugar or not,' she said as she handed Smelly Man three paper sachets and a paddle-pop stick. The man just stood there. Frozen. Evelyn became irritated as she held out the sugar sachets. She looked around and saw that everyone else had frozen too. It was like she was stuck in a land where all the people were frozen in time except her, which was not as pleasant as she thought it would be. She pictured herself wandering through them, pinching Bird Man's nose between her second and third knuckle, dislodging an overall strap off Cartoon Man's shoulder, wiping the surprise smile off Phillip's face, without any of them knowing what had happened when they came to. Perhaps she could even disrobe Smelly Man, hose him down and put him back together again in a new outfit made up of all the extra items from the other frozen people – Phillip's scarf, Cartoon Man's extra jumper – and then when they unfroze, they would wonder how all their clothes magically appeared on Smelly Man. Evelyn laughed, which seemed to rouse the group simultaneously.

'For me?' Smelly Man asked. 'Did you actually get *me* a coffee?' he asked again. Evelyn didn't like incredulity. It usually meant she had done something odd. She tried her guts out to be the same, and when she did something that made her stand out, she always glowed fire engine red. Then she realised he was simply surprised and grateful and, for just a moment, he felt a part of something. That he was more than just a nuisance. Sadness rained from her brain to her toes and tears sat in her eyelids when she saw his happy sooty face.

'Yes, for you,' she said tenderly as she pushed the sugars and stick into his hand. She looked around at the group and saw a mixture of inward shame and outer warmth as past lack of social graces swarmed through them.

'I'm Evelyn,' she said, extending her hand.

'I'm John,' Smelly Man said with a stammer. He had an appropriately firm handshake, and he bowed his head, smiled, and said what a pleasure it was to meet such a wonderful gift-bearing lady with a heart of solid gold. Part of Evelyn thought he went over the top, but most of her thought it a lovely acknowledgement of facts. She didn't quite know what to do with her now sullied hand, but she knew all the goodness would be reversed if she showed any distaste on her face. News of the coffee spread down the queue like a Mexican wave of self-berating and inner promises. It dissipated quickly and the men resumed their dreams of what they would find inside.

'What would you like to find, John?' Bird Man asked. John beamed and spoke of a rare engine he had been trying to find for many years. His head no longer hung low, his shoulders were high, and he told the tale of a train he once had that had been taken from him in his sleep. The group all said that if they saw one before he did, they would be sure to pick it up for him.

'Ten minutes to go,' Cartoon Man in overalls said. Everyone in the line began shaking out their empty bags and lining them over their arms, ready to be filled with goodies. Pockets were patted, loose items secured, up and down movements on the toes to ensure readiness for speed. Glasses were stowed, glasses were brought out and pushed firmly on noses, wallets were checked. Then an eerie quiet flowed through the crowd as they all faced the closed double doors. Evelyn joined in after facing the wrong way for a rebellious few seconds. As always, rebellion for rebellion's sake seemed futile, and she admired the door handles as she stood facing the right way. The thumb-latch pull handles were beautifully plump in the middle and she pictured herself throwing open both doors and entering a cinema from yesteryear – Joan Crawford style, in a full-length strapless number that flowed from the knee.

The doors opened and the crowd pushed through the bottleneck, without a skerrick of regard for others. They ran to the trestle tables inside, full of trains, carriages, tracks and paraphernalia; manned by men who could well have been outside lining up. Evelyn thought these guys must be the elite, the top of their game, and she wondered if Phillip, Bird Man, Cartoon Man and even smelly John dreamed of being the people inside the doors, rather than the train set seagulls squawking around filling their bags with treasure.

Evelyn saw a hip and shoulder that would have landed a man a spot in an elite sports team. Poor John had been shoved aside, but he shook off his shock and went back in. There was a stage at the back of the hall and Evelyn stood on it to look down at the rabble. There were no rules here, and she didn't know whether to admire their gumption or punch them all in the face for being arseholes. When she sat on the edge of the stage, Bird Man dropped a bag next to her and asked if she'd mind it for him.

'You can't leave anything unattended,' he called over his shoulder as he went back into the affray. Before long, Evelyn was minding so many bags, she lost track of whose were whose and she wondered how much trouble she'd get into if she took one item from each bag and placed it in another's bag and so on. Only one way to find out. Evelyn made sure no one was looking each time she swapped a track for a carriage, or a toy station master for a tree, ballast packs for bridge kits and a steam engine for a diesel. She didn't stop at one per bag either. She couldn't stop swapping. There was a brief pause when John came over, holding up a 1926 American Flyer number thirteen passenger set in its original box.

'Well, it certainly is an original box,' Evelyn said. The box, if you could call it that, was faded and frayed. John turned and went back to the crowd, and she wondered where he got his money from. Maybe he was a rich miser. It was lovely that he wanted to show her the engine, she mused, before deciding she might just leave them all to it.

Just as she was standing up to leave, Bird Man came over to add some items to his bag. He looked momentarily confused, which gave Evelyn enough time to walk over to a pillar and stand behind it. She'd been sprung. She went from pillar to pillar and was a third of the way to the door when Bird Man was surrounded by more collectors who began rifling through their bags. Accusations turned to push and shove as the collectors tried to tally what they knew with what was in their bags.

'Stooooop!' Phillip said loudly to the growing group milling about the stage. He began by asking Cartoon Man with overalls what had been in his bag. The group became almost orderly as they handed over items they knew weren't theirs. Evelyn could see a few of them fighting themselves as they handed over something they wanted to claim as their own.

'It was that woman,' one of them said with venom, 'she was minding our bags.' This stopped the group. Evelyn was now the common enemy and she sucked in a deep breath to make herself smaller. The pillar didn't quite hide her, and she willed herself thinner. Phillip explained that it would all sort itself out and returned to a trestle table. The others followed suit, not wanting to miss out on the remaining goods. Phillip made his way over to Evelyn and stood beside the pillar, which provided her the extra cover she needed to remain hidden.

'Not cool, Evelyn,' he said with great power, even though it was under his breath. Evelyn said that she had meant no harm and that she would explain herself later. The pair had arranged for her to go to Phillip's later that evening, to help assemble and place any new items gathered from today's swap meet on his lounge-room train set. 'It's time for you to leave,' Phillip said as he shook his head, 'and tonight is cancelled.'

Evelyn felt sick to the bone as she made her way to the double doors with the plump thumb-latch handles.

CHAPTER NINETEEN

*E*velyn walked as quickly as she could out of the town hall and zigzagged through the streets without care for where she was. The second petrol station she passed had a small walkway at the side of the building. She followed it and tried the door. It was locked. She took a moment to adjust her face because petrol station staff were always reticent to hand over loo keys at the smallest of red flags. When she stood at the counter jiggling and crossing her legs, the man took a glance at her then handed her a key dangling pathetically from the end of a dishevelled wooden spoon big enough to stir a gallon of pasta sauce. Evelyn was so distracted by her own shame that she didn't comment.

Over the years she had taken great amusement in the large items attached to keys in petrol stations or cafés, whose amenities were tucked away down some stairs or at the end of a path to nowhere else. People forget to hand back keys, but they don't forget, nor desire, to keep oversized independently themed fobs. Perhaps, Evelyn thought as she entered the grotty bathroom that hadn't been cleaned since Kennedy got shot, she should carry a children's spade around with her so she could start a series of fob switches. For the briefest of moments, she smiled to herself, but the memory of swapping the carriages and station masters and trees and tracks around caused a lightning rod of gravity through every part of her body.

Evelyn sat on the toilet and let her humiliation course through her. She put her head between her knees and began to sob. Shame kept her doubled over for some time, and she wondered how she would ever be able to walk the streets again. The humiliation was drizzled with an exceptional case of paranoia, and Evelyn pictured every single person in the neighbourhood passing on the rumour of her bad behaviour at the swap meet. Cheryl would shake her head each time she tried to buy a pastry, Bruno would smirk knowingly each time she caught his eye, the nice man at the park would steer Nutmeg in the opposite direction when he saw her, and Don . . . Don would be so disappointed that he would never want to play the banjo for her again. Even Mr Keenan would look down his nose at her when he handed over his stupid shirts.

All Evelyn's past humiliations rattled past her vision like a Japanese bullet train. There were many carriages. Sometimes the train slowed, just to make sure she got a good look inside the carriages. There were small humiliation carriages – where she saw herself waving her arms around wildly at a man who dared to park in a disabled parking spot. She had yelled abuse fuelled by rage at other things until he walked over to a wheelchair and began walking his mother over to the car. The old woman had a crocheted blanket over her lap, and she had produced the permit and waved it at Evelyn. She then explained she had forgotten to leave it in the car and to please not be angry at her son.

'He's a good man,' she had said in so brittle a tone that Evelyn's chest had caved in. There were big ones, too. One carriage slowed down so she could see Little Evelyn pulling out a kitchen drawer in her sleep, and weeing in it because she thought she was in the toilet. Oh, she had never forgotten her mother's drunken laughter when she'd come to. It had become the family party story for so many years.

Evelyn lost her desire to survive, and she decided to sit there for eternity. She would die atop this filthy toilet and be discovered in fifty years. A petrified woman draped in an intact red polyester shirt – her bamboo pants would have disintegrated by then. She thought about writing her epitaph on the grimy subway tiles but decided to save a task for tomorrow. It was important to keep busy. She leaned back against the cistern, and it dug into her back until it hurt. Even then, she refused to sit forward. Instead, she nestled her back further and further into the pain. Maybe this was self-harm, she thought, but dismissed it as self-harm had never been in her repertoire – unless self-punishing thoughts counted. Self-loathing was her specialty, yet so was hubris. She almost wondered whether all people had such inner conflictions, but she was too tired to bother.

Evelyn moved into an adrenaline dump. She knew this because her mouth tasted like rotten socks and iron filings. She had thrown a packet of chewy in her bag before she left that morning because she had been overexcited. Overexcitement never limped to the line, it always crashed into a wall, so she had come prepared. To a degree. Her left calf muscle cramped, and she began hopping around the bathroom, gingerly trying to put weight on her big toe, then her other toe tips, until eventually she could stand on two feet. Rather than use the opportunity to get going, she lay flat on her back on the tiles; even though the grout wasn't black by design.

The cold slowly permeated her skin as she lay there tensing and re-tensing her muscles from her toes to her scalp, trying to put Evelyn Too Far Land into her past. She firmly decided she was not going to starve herself to death in the petrol station toilet. It was Phillip's loss. She was a good friend and interesting company, and she wasn't going to be brought down by a man in a beige suit with a western star belt buckle. Perhaps he should take a look in the mirror before casting aspersions and passing judgement on her. And, even when she couldn't do anything for herself, Evelyn was very good at mustering for others. The picture was bigger than her and she had a delightful boy and his sad mother to get back to.

But she couldn't stand up just yet. Her body felt like it was being pulled down, and that if it kept lowering itself, there would be calm at the end. It became heavier and heavier as it descended to the earth's core a millimetre at a time. Calm, rest, sleep, so tantalisingly close. A patchy sleep set in and she became a mould caterpillar that slowly made its way through grout troughs until it hurled itself over a tile ledge and hit a smooth surface. As she gained speed she morphed into a shivering mouse with a twitchy nose. The mouse sneezed and she blew up into a cat who rolled his shoulders over at each sound, his fur puffed out to make himself look bigger to oncoming prey.

Evelyn's body jerked awake. Her head had slipped back, her mouth was open and dry. It was lucky she was behind a locked door, or someone may just mistake her for a ceramic clown at the show and try to put a ping-pong ball in her mouth and expect a stuffed toy. She coughed and spluttered and slowly creaked her neck back until it was straight, before opening and closing her mouth a few times to prevent lockjaw. She had no idea how long she had been asleep but there was certainly no miraculous power-nap rejuvenation.

Evelyn rolled her shoulders and slowly made her way onto her side, then into the crawl position before hoisting herself up with the toilet. A few seconds of dizzy lapsed, and she braved a look in the piece of stainless-steel pretending to be a mirror. It contorted her face so it looked like an hourglass; big buggy eyes at the top with a Joker's smile in the base.

Her nose made the bottleneck, and her feelings were the sand specs making their way from her brain to the nausea in her stomach. There was no point telling herself to pull herself together, but her naturally optimistic spirit did it anyway. She took some thin barely-there toilet paper sheets, wet them and wiped her face with the gelatinous paper ball, then dusted herself off and headed back to the laundromat.

God knows where she was going to take herself that night. She had told Cheryl all about her train play date, and she didn't want her neighbour to see the lights on above the laundromat. To see that it had been cancelled. Perhaps she could pack some snacks and hide under a tree for a few hours.

CHAPTER TWENTY

*E*velyn left at the time she would have if she'd been going to Phillip's to play trains. Her body took her to Don's, and she rapped on the door after pacing up and down his verandah a few times. For courage.

'Hello,' Don said when he opened the door.

'I've had the worst day, Don,' she said as she followed him inside. Instead of going out the back, he walked into the lounge room on the left. There was a record playing. Evelyn watched it turn around and around, and found herself mesmerised by the needle. How these discs worked had always been a mystery to her. Don sat on the couch, and she sat in the armchair next to the record player. When she tore herself away from record watching and told him the tale of the swap meet, she didn't even get annoyed when he laughed along at the images of chaos as everyone tried to scramble to find what was rightfully theirs. As she recapped, she found it funny too, but her voice became sombre when she told him that Phillip didn't want to play with her anymore. And that she was supposed to be there that night, and she didn't want Don to think she had no friends.

'I'm your friend,' Don said. It was the kindness that did her in, and Evelyn launched into her mini breakdown in the petrol station toilet. She even told him about turning into a mould caterpillar that morphed into a cat in her foggy half stress sleep. When she looked up, she was pleased to find he had the right look on his face. It wasn't sympathetic, nor astounded, which would have made her feel alone. It was just his danger-free face.

'Let's have a wine,' he said, leaving the room to get a bottle. She felt bad for not bringing something, but it had taken all her strength to simply knock on his door. She looked around while he was gone and noticed the sheer curtains over the front window. He would have seen her pacing up and down the verandah, yet he hadn't said anything about it.

The bookshelf to the left of the fireplace was distinctly lacking in books. She usually found bookless shelves sad but, instead, there was a lovely array of things that took Evelyn back to the past. There were two original telephones, back when you had to dial each number all the way around, with their tightly curled cords. She thought of the woman in the pool team with her boingy Tigger tight curls for a moment and smiled ruefully. The way the group had turned on Andy and Molly still rankled her; they'd done nothing wrong.

Evelyn's eyes found a curved wooden box and she lifted the lid. It was full of tickets to concerts – one each. Don wasn't so different to her, she supposed, going around the world alone. She didn't think much of the bands – who on earth went to Kiss concerts? – but she liked that the stubs were all neatly preserved in a lovely box lined with rich dark red felt.

'Do you remember Fuzzy Felts?' she asked when she felt Don in the room. When he said no, she told him of the themed boxes full of colourful felt cut-outs. Her favourite had been the farm one, and she had spent hours as a child making different agricultural worlds where she could almost smell the cow poo as she imagined herself running around paddocks patting the cows and the sheep.

'For a while, I wanted to be a dairy farmer when I grew up,' she said in conclusion. Don laughed and said it was not a romantic occupation. 'Well, neither is a paint shop or a laundromat,' she said with a smile. She had been facing his shelf since he had returned to the room. He had delicately placed a glass of wine on a spare bit of shelf and had let her be. For some reason she felt small. Too fragile to meet his eye. When her brain was ready, she turned back around, sat down, and wound her legs up under herself.

'That shelf is my memory drawer,' Don said.

'Mine's not a memory drawer, it a drawer of things past.' Don didn't quibble. He had an uncanny ability to pick his battles, but she went on a defensive rant anyway. Keeping history was not the same as storing things that drew the mind to relive the past.

Don spent some time saying how refreshing he found her company.

'When I'm with you,' he said, cocking his head to the side, 'I feel like I actually matter.'

Evelyn sat there dumbfounded for a moment. Her natural reaction to compliments was to hurl insults to fend them off. To deflect them from entering her being. She saw herself in a bright green field, the sun blasting, the sky the blue fire engines would be if fire engines were blue. She stood ramrod straight with a round golden metal shield that reflected mammoth targeted rays back at her opposition. Her golden wrist bands, knee bands and ankle-high brown leather boots all matched her brown leather tunic. The helmet sitting proudly on her head had metal sideburns and a piece coming down the centre of her face to protect her nose. She brandished her sword and prepared for the oncoming enemy, then, without warning, she sheathed her sword and walked away from battle. The sun goddess's deep sultry voice echoed around inside her helmet: 'This was not a fight – not today.'

So, she didn't hurl insults when the compliment met her ears. Instead, she let the statement ferment in the air between them. He was looking out the window without expectation. She flitted between thinking Don must be such a sad little man if she made him feel like he mattered, and feeling like she had a fever coming on – because if she made him feel like he mattered, then maybe, just maybe, she mattered.

Evelyn stood up and walked over to Don, extended her hand and pulled him up out of his chair. They hugged. The affection swooshed through her like a throat drowning in warm tea, and her mind and body whirled in confusion at her newfound determination to see a hug through to the end. Instead of putting up a force field against these feelings, she closed her eyes and rested her cheek on Don's shoulder. The hug enveloped her and she could hear a waterfall. Like the one she saw on a day trip to Trentham one day. She had climbed over the fence, gingerly made her way down to the bottom of the waterfall and walked under it. There she stood, arms out, while the thunderous sound of the water gushed down mere centimetres from her face. She was back there. The sound was bigger than her ear pipes, which strained to cope with the deluge. Evelyn let out a Mount Vesuvius hiccup and thanked her body for giving her a reason to pull away from the hug. So there was no embarrassment for either of them. They gave each other an elbow squeeze as a gesture of thanks, found a little mirth at the loudest hiccup the world had ever heard and sat back down in their respective chairs.

Don picked up his banjo and started strumming. Evelyn wondered how he could play so many notes that had absolutely no connection to each other at all. This was his hiccup.

It put a line through the hug, and they moved forward. Don began bellowing a song, completely out of tune, about how much he loved playing the banjo.

'I looooove playing the banjooooooo,' he sang, running the 'o' until he was out of breath, 'espeshshshsaleeeee for Evelynnnnnnnnnnnn. Sheeeee makes me happppyyyyyyy.' While Don stream-of-consciousnessed, Evelyn sat there thinking how simply marvellous it was to have a song written about her and let his loud, unabashed out-of-tune swooning fill her right up until the meniscus in her brain burst.

Evelyn laughed, gave him a standing ovation and cheered like she hadn't since she saw the sad clown at the circus when she was seven. He had ridden his wonky bike around the ring between the acts that received most of the attention, barely able to push the peddles as he looked around at the crowd with exaggerated inner turmoil. Evelyn had loved that clown, and thought perhaps he was another major inspiration for all her face practising. Although she hid her face from Don on occasion, she realised she didn't have to care about her expressions when she was with him. Every now and then her face slipped into the deepest parts of herself and, whenever it did, he looked at her with a smile, with kindness, with that stupid grin. And underlying all these responses, there was genuine affection for her. Come to think of it, she had a genuine affection for him.

He excused himself for a moment after placing his banjo back on its stand. Evelyn thought she might ask whether he was ever going to have any actual lessons when he got back, but instead she picked up her bag, patted herself down to make sure she had everything, and went whistling all the way home.

CHAPTER TWENTY-ONE

*E*velyn nearly dropped her iron when she heard the bell on her stable-style door ledge ring. The old bell that had come with the laundromat had barely got her attention, so when she had spotted a large brass desk bell with a base the size of an old 45 record in the local junk store, she had seized the opportunity. Although she didn't normally go for swirling floral etchings on anything, she had found her fingers running across the patterns and she let them do what they wanted for a change. But the new bell sure was loud. She took the briefest of moments to recover from the sound, brought herself back from her imaginings and turned around with her most welcoming smile. She was so surprised to see Phillip standing there that she let out an 'Ooooff' before she could stop herself. He was wearing his full suit, despite the warm day, and Evelyn turned away with a burning red face.

'I'm sorry about cancelling our train date,' he said.

Evelyn tried to stop her bubbling hurt from reaching the front of her face. She certainly wasn't going to tell him about nearly dying in the petrol station toilet.

Phillip went on to explain that, although there had been quite a raucous going on when she left the swap meet, everyone had begun listening to each other quite quickly. When someone said they were missing something, the others would look for the items in their bags. Before too long, all the items had been returned to the rightful owners.

'The best thing, Evelyn, was that everyone in the room then knew what everyone else craved and instead of pushing and fighting and clamouring for what they wanted, they all started finding items that they knew the others were after.'

Evelyn looked at Phillip; her face almost concealed her growing delight.

'So, you brought everyone together. Thank you,' he said sincerely with a broad open smile.

Evelyn was full to the brim of vindication, so she offered him a cup of tea. Phillip accepted the offer and she ushered him through to the small table in the kitchen and put up the cardboard clock she had bought recently. It had lovely big fat hands that were visible from the front door and she displayed it whenever she had to go out or close the stable door. The numbers were in a clear plain font and she set it for fifteen minutes from now.

'So, everyone decided that perhaps they should get together and hire out the mechanics' institute in a town less than an hour away. They're going to bring any unwanted items they have in their collections and swap them with each other and share their hobby instead of fighting. Would you like to come?' he asked.

Well, yes, she would, but she would have to check her growing calendar entries upstairs and get back to him. Although the outcome from the swap meet had turned out well, she was still very embarrassed by what she'd done. If someone had come into the laundromat and swapped items in the full wash service bags, it would take her weeks to work out who needed what sock or what have you.

'In the meantime, perhaps you could come over and check on your hay bales,' Phillip said. 'I have some rocks to paint, too.' He stood up and said he would leave her to think about things. She opened up her stable door and returned to her tasks with a lighter step.

Evelyn managed three hours before she rang Phillip and agreed to go over that very night. When she arrived, she presented him with a Tupperware container of small hard muffins she had made after work. They were edible if drunk with a cup of tea, she explained, as she set about making them one. She didn't bother looking in the mugs, she knew they'd be grubby. They'd go just perfectly with almost muffins. They sat on the two stools alongside his train set and laboured their way through tea that hadn't had enough time to brew and muffins they could almost chew.

'I like a little tea in my milk,' Phillip said presently. They both giggled and Evelyn wiped a soggy bit of muffin she'd accidentally spat out off the train set grass and wiped it on her jeans. She liked that there were no pretences between them. After they had forced down two muffins each, Evelyn explained that she needed to become a cook now that she practically had a family. When they stood to play, Phillip gave Evelyn the honours. She turned on the train set and the lights. Phillip crawled under the table and popped up through a hatch in the far fields so he could pull down the blinds on the window. For atmosphere.

'It's night-time in the village,' Evelyn said in her best suspenseful television voiceover. She employed a British accent.

'It's an American village in 1954,' Phillip said, looking a little surprised that she thought it was anywhere else. He had matched the era perfectly to a particular year, a particular village, a particular season and was flummoxed that she thought they were in Britain. He began to point out the tell-tale signs. Evelyn didn't much care for his version and dismissed him.

'It doesn't matter where it is,' she said, 'but, look, here comes the train to the station and Mr Higginbotham is alighting to go home to his hobby farm –' Evelyn began.

'That's not Mr Higginbotham,' Phillip said, keeping his indignance to a minimum, 'that's Mr Southerly.'

'Men with red pants aren't called Mr Southerly,' Evelyn said, floored by his lack of logic.

Phillip chose to stay quiet for a few moments and let her pick up the red-panted man and waddle him over to a small cottage, but he couldn't stay quiet for long.

'No, he lives in the big house. He's the landowner and spent the day in town at the bank discussing his financial investments,' he said in a clipped tone.

'No, he went to town for a cash job bricklaying. The farm is failing, and he needs to top up his income,' she said, slowing her voice like she was talking to a child who wouldn't listen properly. 'And, look, this is his wife,' she added, picking up a woman from a nearby property and plonking her in the yard of the small cottage. 'She makes bread and sells it to the surrounding houses to top up their income.' She didn't mention that she had seen herself as the wide-skirted woman when she had baked the muffins earlier that day. Not that she had to do anything but add water to the premix box she had bought at the supermarket. Half price because of the looming use-by date.

Phillip picked up the wide-skirted woman and put her back where she belonged.

'No, she's standing outside enjoying the fresh air after a rich dinner. See, she lives at the big house, she's Mr Southerly's mother-in-law and she's gloating because she got her way earlier today,' he said as he sat back down. It was time to take a break from the growing tension between them.

Evelyn sat back down too.

'I don't want to fight,' she said. She had been so excited to come over and play with Phillip, and here they were bickering over dreams. Although, she supposed, one defended dreams more than real life, where acquiescence abounded. She had finally met someone who also saw alternative worlds, or at least shared them out loud, and there they were wasting this most precious opportunity to meld worlds. She had imagined there was no bigger bond, and yet . . .

'Let's take it in turns,' Phillip said in a low, warm voice. Evelyn thought this was a terrific idea and suggested they do the 1954 American town before the ye olde British village, and so Phillip stood and introduced Evelyn to his people, his houses, his town. He explained who was having affairs with who while Evelyn stated, 'Oh, how controversial,' and made the odd embellishment to their lives.

Phillip spoke about the unhappy housewife who had caved to family pressures and married a man she didn't like. As time passed, the couple had settled into their lives and created a façade for their families while they each took secret lovers. The woman advised her husband on business matters and his career had skyrocketed. She was happy taking credit out of the limelight. He had become tender as time had gone on and a child was born, who looked a little more like the local butcher than the husband. It was a girl who would go on to study at university, forge a career and live the life her mother hadn't quite dared to.

Then Evelyn took the reins and spoke of the British village. It was a simpler place where there were no affairs or inner discontent because some people, Evelyn explained, just love growing pumpkins, showing pumpkins at the local fair, cooking pumpkins and eating pumpkin soup for dinner every day for twelve and a half years.

'Because it doesn't matter what your passion is,' she said to Phillip as she lovingly stroked the plastic head of her pumpkin farmer, 'as long as you own it and don't listen to anybody else's judgement.' After her dairy farming phase, all Little Evelyn had wanted to be when she grew up was a shopkeeper. When she played imaginations in her bedroom, each prop, each setting had been markets, stores, shopping strips and village general stores. She supposed, as she looked back, it was because Mr Hennessy at her local milk bar had been so warm and kind. He had let her go behind the counter at times to fill the little white paper bags with mixed lollies at her own discretion. She did this down low to the ground and, when the odd kid had come in to buy a bag, she would hand it up to Mr Hennessy who would give it to the child who would whoop in delight when they saw something they liked in the bag.

At the conclusion of the tour of her village, she told Phillip of her cold parents who couldn't be less interested in their daughter, and explained how she had taken herself away to imaginary lands where parents were warm and cuddly.

When it was time for her to go home, they grasped each other's elbows and nodded with warmth in their eyes. Evelyn was pleased that she hadn't stormed out over the little fuss about the location of the village. The different villages they each had ensconced in their heads; the differing places they went for differing reasons. Because it was nice to dream together. Differently.

CHAPTER TWENTY-TWO

*E*velyn looked across when the desk bell rang the next day, and a surge of panic rang through her core. It was one of the teachers she had seen around the schoolyard when she had picked Ben up recently.

'Hello,' the teacher said in a clipped tone with a smile that didn't reach her eyes. The woman was clearly doing her best to portray an outward calm. Her teeth weren't quite clenched, but her outside demeanour wasn't strong enough to stop some stress from rising to the surface. 'Ben has spoken about you, in fact he did a drawing recently and told me that the lady and the man either side of him were you and Don from the paint shop,' she continued with a forced slowness. For a millisecond, Evelyn filled with chuff, but she returned to concern just as quickly.

'Has something happened?' Evelyn asked, mirroring the teacher's demeanour.

'Well, I was wondering if he happened to be here,' the teacher said, almost casually.

'No,' Evelyn said as she came out through the stable-style door and locked up without thought of her cardboard clock.

'He's run away from school, and I can't get June on the phone. We have people out looking and I thought I'd start here. Do you know where he might have gone?' Evelyn shook her head, told the teacher she'd help look and then ran down the street.

Evelyn was struggling to think logically as her body took her to the park where they kicked the soccer ball and patted Nutmeg. Nothing. Next stop Don's house. Nothing. No one was home, so Evelyn inelegantly scaled the five-foot gate at the side of Don's house and scanned the backyard. Worry aided her climbing skills. Still nothing. She thought briefly about heading to Ben and June's flat, but she knew in her belly that he wouldn't be there. Besides, the teacher would most likely go there and wasting resources wasn't prudent. Evelyn meandered a couple of local streets trying desperately to think where an eight-year-old boy would go. Every now and then she heard Ben's name being called. Instead of thinking about where an eight-year-old boy would go, she started to explore where she would go if she had run away and was frightened of getting into trouble.

Evelyn thought back to the time she ran away from the annual family reunion when she was around Ben's age. Her cousins were a tight solid group whose sole entertainment for the day was to tease her endlessly, mercilessly. Little Evelyn knew she wasn't a poo face who cried wee tears, or a stupid motherfucker, or a ten-tonne freckle-head booger, but as she stood there surrounded by the bigger kids whirling around her in a circle so tight that she couldn't break free, she had begun to wonder whether the ringing in her ears was going to blow her brain up. When the kids got hungry and left her standing there, full of fraught, she made her way over to a trestle table, lifted up the front of her dress and began filling the dress pouch she'd made with potato chips.

Little Evelyn had held the hem up tight and made her way to the second closest park. She lay under the slide with just her eyes out, watched the sun go down and the stars come out. Each chip was placed on her tongue one at a time until it became so mushy she could squeeze the chip pulp through the gaps in her teeth before swallowing it. She looked at the night sky and saw herself as a grown-up astronaut floating from star to star in her helmet and puffy spacesuit. Out in space, she didn't have to look at or hear anyone. A place where she could just be herself, and be free of the poison word-arrows that barraged her daily on earth.

Evelyn remembered hearing people calling her name when they'd come looking for her. She had been so scared of being punished that she had stayed quiet and shrunk herself as much as she could under the slide. Silent tears had fallen down her face and, even though they tickled and she needed to scratch her face, she had stayed balled up ever so tightly where the slide met the ground. She had barely breathed until the voices that called her name had disappeared. Then she had developed a plan. She would sneak back into the family get-together, pretend she had been there all along and reveal herself with a 'What is this fuss all about?' face. Plans don't always work out, including this one, and Little Evelyn had been frogmarched to the car and pushed into the back seat as her parents continually apologised to family members for the inconvenience she had caused. She had cried and bleated about the horrible mean cousins and was told that, unlike her, they were fine children, and that she needed to develop a backbone.

Evelyn began to look for Ben in all available hidey-holes. When she got to the carpark full of utes and tradie cars next to the monstrosity apartment building being erected at the end of the main street, she turned in and began looking around and under the cars. The smallest crescent of a soccer ball peeked out from behind the rear wheel of a large dirty red tray ute, and Evelyn stealthily made her way around to the other side of the car. There was Ben, crouched between the back tyres of two cars with the soccer ball at his feet. He was gripping onto it tightly; his face was hidden between his knees.

Evelyn knelt down on the gravel even though the stones dug into her knees. There was no way that sharp stones embedding themselves into her skin could compare to the pain coursing through young Ben's body, so how dare she even wince.

'Hello, darling,' Evelyn said, softly and kindly as a tear fell out of her left eye. She wondered why her left eye always leaked first. Ben looked up with a face full of fear that softened as soon as he realised it was Evelyn. He burst into tears. His tears came out of both eyes at the same time; apparently Evelyn's eyes were an anomaly.

'How about we just sit here for a minute and take a few breaths,' she added, shifting from her knees to her bottom in an awkward half roll. Stones in her bum were much better than stones in her knees.

Evelyn dusted the knee stones away and picked out the remaining few that had embedded in her skin. Ben relaxed his body a little and brought the soccer ball up to his chest. He held it like his life depended on it. A voice calling his name passed by the front of the carpark and they both sat there in silence looking at each other. Evelyn brought her index finger up to her lips to indicate a shoosh and Ben nodded with a small smile that had fought its way to the corners of his mouth. Evelyn's mouth followed suit without permission and, within a few seconds, they were beaming conspiratorially at each other.

When the voice calling Ben's name had disappeared, Evelyn leaned forward so he could hear her whispering.

'I have a secret spot not too far from here, it's dirty and gross but it's a perfect place to sit and eat an ice-cream while we work out what to do about this little pickle you're in,' Evelyn said in a medium whisper with her hands around her mouth to stop the whisper from hopping on a bit of errant breeze and carrying to one of the people calling his name.

'I don't like pickles,' Ben said right back, mimicking the whisper volume and the hand motion.

'Me neither, darling. Shall we?' she asked. Ben nodded, stood up to hunchback position so his head didn't poke up above the car line and shuffled over to Evelyn. He put the soccer ball down and reached out both hands to help her up. First go saw him fall into her lap, second go saw him plant his feet a little more firmly, and Evelyn tried harder to hoist herself up. Third go was a charm and they stood in hunchback position together. They both rubbed their bums to dislodge the stubborn stones before Evelyn poked her eyes over the tray of the ute to make sure the coast was clear. It was, and they made their way to the petrol station where the bathroom hadn't been cleaned since Kennedy was shot.

CHAPTER TWENTY-THREE

Outside the petrol station, Evelyn explained that she and Ben would go inside, pick an ice-cream each and, when they got to the counter, Ben was to say, 'I need to go to the toilet, Auntie.'

'I don't have an auntie,' Ben said. He elongated the first syllable. Evelyn tucked a wayward curl behind his ear and felt a little foolish. She chastised herself for her innate ability to turn even obtaining a toilet key into a major event and suggested they eliminate the auntie bit and just say the toilet bit. A half drama was indicative of self-improvement on the fly, and she gave herself a silent back pat.

When they entered the shop, Ben ran straight to the ice-creams as though the morning hadn't happened at all. There were too many choices, but he eventually settled on a Bubble O'Bill because it had a nose chewy; which meant he got two for one.

'I need to go to the toilet, Auntie Evie,' Ben said as she paid. Evelyn shrugged at the petrol station man, and he flopped the key tied to the wooden spoon onto the counter. They made their way down the path beside the large gas tanks and headed into the bathroom. Evelyn put the toilet lid down, wet some thin paper into a pulp ball and wiped the top of the lid so Ben could sit. He shook his head and gestured that she should sit instead, which put them at equal eye height as he leaned back against the basin and carefully opened his ice-cream wrapper.

Ben blew into its protective bag and pulled it out without any ice-cream touching the sides. This pleased him and Evelyn followed suit. She wondered why she had never thought of this herself. If she added up all the bits of ice-cream that had stuck to the wrappers over the years, she'd have an ice-cream lake to swim in.

Evelyn put all her strength into stopping herself from fidgeting or speaking. If she could just wait him out, perhaps he'd start talking.

'I did a dumb thing, Evie,' Ben said when he was down to the cowboy's ice-cream eyes. The hat had been chocolate and he had a brown ring around his lips.

'We all do dumb things from time to time, Ben. If I made a list of all the dumb things I did, the piece of paper would wrap around the world twice,' Evelyn said. It probably would, too, she thought to herself and snickered unexpectedly. Some of her ice-cream mouthful went up through her head, instead of down, and landed uncomfortably in the top of her nose.

As she mopped her watering eye and dabbed at her leaking nose, Ben told her how he had played pass the parcel at a birthday party back when he used to get invited to them. Last night, he had an idea when his mum was resting her eyes. He had snuck over to the milk crate in which his mother kept her only ring and wrapped it in a small square of newspaper. The ring was gold and his mum always kept it tucked away. Ben had put fifteen more wrappings around it and still even had some sticky tape left for emergencies by the time it was finished, and then he put it in his school bag.

'And some of the kids wanted to play and came into the library, even though some kids thought pass the parcel was for babies,' he said before licking the stick clean for the third time. Evelyn did not understand this, as she liked the lingering taste of ice-cream in her mouth rather than the bitter wood taste from the stick. Throughout his monologue, Evelyn had nodded and hmm-hmmed in all the right places, and she put the chocolate waffle cone end of her Drumstick into her mouth to let it melt. 'And Petey had his back turned and hummed the Simpson tune, and when it stopped on the final round, Max and his friends came into the library and just took it. And when Max opened the last piece of paper in front of everyone, he held up the ring and said it was for girls and we were all a bunch of sissies.' Ben's voice had gotten quicker and his eyes wider as he spoke. Evelyn noted there was a tremble in his hand.

'And then I said it's not for sissies, it was my mum's ring, and he said I was going to get my arse kicked and then he kicked me in the stomach and now I don't know what to do. I don't want Mum to be mad at me,' he said as he crouched down and sat on the floor under the basin. Evelyn stood up and held out her hands to him as he had to her when they rose from behind the tray ute. She wished she could take the knot in his stomach and put it in her own as she pulled him upright, drew him into her middle and let him cry while her mind whizzed around trying to clutch one of the solutions flying around her. The image of herself pushing Max up against a wall and forcibly taking the ring from him came around more than the others and she scrunched her eyes closed as tight as she could so the idea had nothing to stick to. This was not the solution, even though it was the solution.

Evelyn didn't make promises, even ones she could keep, but she told him they had to face the music. Because that is just how it goes.

'The more you face the music, the easier it becomes,' Evelyn said. The lie had tumbled out effortlessly.

'Maybe if I tell the teacher, she can get the ring back off Max?' Ben asked. Evelyn saw hope cascading through his face, and she wondered when her well of hope had become so barren that it had closed for business. Forever.

'Or actually,' he said with a very serious face, 'I will just say I'm sorry and I was upset, and I don't know why I ran away and I promise I won't do it again.' Again, the pace of his words increased, but not due to fraught this time; resolve had bubbled through his muddy pickle. He reiterated his plan, put his hand in Evelyn's and together they went to face the music.

CHAPTER TWENTY-FOUR

*L*ater that week, the bell on the stable-style door ledge rang again. Evelyn looked up from her ironing and saw June standing there. Aside from being dishevelled, she sported a spectacular black eye. It was a deep, rich, royal family purple with red raised blotches scattered over it. Evelyn immediately thought of fairy bread. Burst red capillaries fanned through the white of June's eye underneath a milky film umbrella. Evelyn couldn't take her eyes off it as she dropped her iron and took three quick steps towards her. June placed her forearms on the stable-door ledge, and Evelyn took her hands in her own. June twitched with sobs she couldn't quite suppress while Evelyn waited.

'I can't do this anymore, I wanted it to be different for Ben. I didn't want him to have my life,' June said in staggered syllables. Evelyn's chest fell in on itself.

'Let's go upstairs,' Evelyn said as she edged June through the door and closed it behind her. She quickly stood her cardboard clock and iron up and followed June closely on the stairs so she could cushion her fall, should she topple.

June blurted. She told Evelyn how she had gone to her mate's place and things had gotten out of hand. They'd all taken speed. Rather than bonding like they normally did, the fractures and fissures in between them became grand canyons. Instead of having fun, they yelled and fought, and June had pushed a wardrobe over. It had landed on Fat Wally who, when he eventually climbed out from underneath it, belted her square in the face. June had fought back and, before she knew it, she was on the ground being kicked. She lifted up her jumper and turned around. There was a big cherry bruise the size of a cricket ball on the outside of her kidneys. Evelyn reeled on the inside but kept her outsides frozen in time.

June then explained there was no need for a lecture, her precursor to the admission that she'd left Ben alone for the whole night. Evelyn bristled but knew she wouldn't be able to contain herself much longer. Especially if she remained stationary.

'What am I going to doooooo?' June wailed into her hands.

'Well, you haven't had any sleep, so let's put you to bed,' Evelyn said with enough authority to induce compliance, but not enough to spark rebellion. She walked June into her room, knelt down and undid June's shoelaces. June shrank to the smallest size she could and let Evelyn lie her down. They had a brief conversation about Evelyn collecting Ben from school and Evelyn said that she would camp with Ben in the living room.

'It'll be fun,' she said, 'and he'll feel safe knowing you're having a sleepover too.' The words came out soothingly, but her heart was icy. This was a right royal mess. She asked June for her house key and said she'd pick up some things for them both. June didn't argue and closed her eyes while Evelyn was still making her rather long list of plans. Evelyn also told June about Ben losing her ring that she kept in a special spot, and not to be too cross with him because he already felt worse than she could imagine. She wasn't sure if June was asleep or not, but if the ring's disappearance ever popped up again, she would be able to say June had been dutifully informed.

Evelyn went back downstairs and opened her stable door again. Perhaps her regular customers wondered why the most reliable businesswoman in the street had begun closing sporadically for no apparent reason. At least she had her cardboard clock to inform people. She loved it much more than she knew she ought to.

She got as much done as she could before heading off to pick up Ben. They'd be back well before the late afternoon pickups, and she set off with purpose.

When Evelyn spied Ben coming through the school gates, he seemed resigned. Small, thin, discouraged – not unlike his mother. He smiled when he saw Evelyn waving enthusiastically and he ran over with delight. He threw his arms around her middle and Evelyn stood there patting his back ever so lightly, to let him know she was right there without smothering him. She had no idea where all her balance and grace had come from, but she was very proud of herself as they walked back to the laundromat. She told him his mum was fine, that she was asleep in Evelyn's bed (Ben stopped for a few seconds and looked up to seek facial confirmation of this most unlikely turn of events) and that they were going to pick up some things from his home and have a sleepover in Evelyn's lounge room after dinner.

And so, the unlikely pair packed some overnight things at Ben's house and headed back to the laundromat. After some serious snacking, Evelyn took Ben upstairs and folded out the sofa bed. He unpacked the three toys he'd brought with him and some colouring pencils. She gave him the option of staying up there or coming down to the formica table in the laundromat – which he picked without hesitation. She finished off her jobs behind the stable door while he did some drawings and coloured in at the table. Evelyn patiently rattled off items from a house, a car, a beach and a soccer field to his seemingly endless question 'What should I draw?' He showed her each picture on completion and helped customers carry their washing baskets to their cars. There were few other words. They just were: a washerwoman and a neighbourhood boy whiling away the time.

For three days and three nights, Evelyn and Ben trudged through uncertainty under the pretence that everything was fine. The elephant in the room moved from Evelyn's bed to the couch somewhere on day one and, in the brief moments June was awake, Evelyn and/or Ben handed her water, tea and light food. June chewed with her mouth open and stared vacantly as she battled to eat. Occasionally, she would smooth Ben's hair tenderly, or pass Evelyn a small smile laced with gratitude. When she spoke, it was in rhyme and made sense on the odd occasion.

Evelyn was grateful to have her bed back but spent most of her sleeping hours on hyper alert, waking to the smallest of sounds. She was pleased that Ben seemed to pass out like he'd run a marathon each day. He was going through the motions, but concern creased his forehead when he sat and stared at his mum. Evelyn had taught him Chinese chequers, and they had taken to sitting there in silent play. She wondered whether he would regain his curiosity, his chatter, his bounce. There were moments of glee, though, when he did a seven or eight stage marble jump, or landed a marble in the very end of the triangle. He always chose blue, she yellow.

The marbles had light veins running through them and Evelyn imagined miners finding gold veins in the rocks; a victorious thread that made all the hours underground worthwhile. Each time they played, she saw herself and Ben beneath a mine in olden-day clothes, working twelve-hour days with a five-minute break each four hours. They would sit and eat their Cornish pasties, meat at one end, raspberry the other. Evelyn suggested they go to Sovereign Hill one day, when Ben's mum got better, and Ben lit up at the thought of a future. But he self-suppressed quite quickly. Unlike her, he couldn't afford to dream in his shitshow of a life.

Evelyn had also suggested going to Don's to play soccer and have a barbeque.

'What if Mum wakes up?' Ben said as he pushed himself down in his seat.

'Then she wakes up,' Evelyn said.

'What if she thinks she's alone?' Ben asked with a sharp edge in his tone. His arms were pushed out straight, downpipes for the flood of feelings that needed to escape his body. Evelyn sat back in her chair with no idea of what to do or say. So, she didn't.

CHAPTER TWENTY-FIVE

*A*nd just like that, the three days and three nights were over. June sat up on the couch with wide open eyes and a mouth like an 'O'. It only took a few seconds for her to take in her surroundings, flick her eyes between Ben and Evelyn and then smile, albeit sheepishly. Ben ran over and gave her a hug while Evelyn passed through a string of emotions. Seeing them hug made her warm, a pop of resentment brought acid up her throat, relief dropped her shoulders, and a dash of outrage made her skull tingle. She fanned her face with her hands, gathered her insides together and harnessed her organisational skills.

The trio sat through an edible dinner of warmed-up takeaway leftovers and small talk. They skirted around the obvious for the sake of the child. When Evelyn's periphery caught the golden glow of the surrounding homes through the window, she imagined all the people sitting around their tables doing the exact same thing. At least they were filling the silence. No one had bothered during her childhood dinners, not even Evelyn in the end. When Ben asked why she had laughed at nothing, she said she was just so pleased to have such wonderful company.

After Ben went to sleep, the two women went downstairs to have a chat out of earshot. June became smaller and smaller as they descended the stairs and by the time they sat at the formica table with a cup of tea, she had shrunk so far inside herself that Evelyn's high horse took flight and bolted into the ether.

What happened next surprised them both. June had been on her last warning at work, and the three days and three nights without even a phone call put her head firmly on the chopping block. As June's eyes moistened, Evelyn smiled and said how fortuitous this was given how busy she had become of late. When she told June how often she had put up her cardboard clock showing an approximate return time, June said that between them perhaps they'd be reliable and giggled at her own joke. Evelyn thrust a smile through her mortification to hide her severe discomfort. The comparison had slapped her sideways, yet she couldn't deny the truth of it. So, they clinked teacups, toasted tight ships and headed off for Evelyn's tour of June's new workplace.

As she strode around and pointed at the lint filters in the dryer (important to clean them daily), the congealed lumps of sodden detergent around the tops of the washers (also important to clean daily), the cardboard inserts for Mr Keenan's shirts (they could worry about his needs tomorrow), the allocated spaces for full-service wash pickups (labelling everything clearly was the key to short sharp delivery) and the day kitchenette (going upstairs not recommended due to potential theft during long absences), Evelyn found the opportunity to puncture in some awkward questions that would have left them both on their back feet had they been eye to eye at the formica table.

Between the dryers and the washing machines, Evelyn suggested, perhaps, that her name could be put down at the school as an approved person to pick up Ben. Evelyn could see that June accepted her logic by the way she tilted her head and pushed her bottom lip right up into her top one, which left June's chin full of tiny mini dimples as she nodded. Good. Between the washing machines and Mr Keenan's cardboard inserts, she asked why June took drugs in the first place. June said it was fun, until it wasn't, and Evelyn was able to suppress her surprise at such an inadequate response by focusing both their attentions on the full-service wash storage space.

When Evelyn finished her explanation of the storage space, June threw in a thank you for everything as she stroked the thick canvas sacks that the local kindergarten used to transport the endless dirty bibs, face washers and tea towels. Evelyn gave June's elbow a small squeeze, muttered a 'you're welcome' and proceeded to point out the kitchenette items, even though the toaster was clearly a toaster, the kettle clearly a kettle and the small under-bench fridge was clearly a fridge. Evelyn said the rest could wait for the morning and the two women headed back upstairs a little taller than they'd been on the way down.

When they got to the lounge room, June whispered that she would put Evelyn's name down at the school in the morning. Evelyn said that there was no hurry to go home, and perhaps staying another couple of days to let the dust settle may be in order. June was momentarily taken aback and whispered that they could talk about it in the morning. Evelyn saw a wave of exhaustion pass over June's face, nodded vigorously and flapped her hands to indicate that nothing really mattered at all.

As Evelyn lay her head down for the night, she saw blue skies, herself arriving for Sunday lunch and sitting on the squeaky chair at the table that should have been thrown out years ago to watch Don, June and Ben playing cricket in the backyard of their new family home.

CHAPTER TWENTY-SIX

*E*velyn rose with the birds, tiptoed past her sleeping guests and went straight to Don's house. It was too early, but she wanted to catch him before he left for work and make sure she returned to the laundromat in time for opening. She walked three times around Don's block before she was ready to ring the doorbell. The light had been on in his lounge room a second time around the block, but she threw in an extra lap to give him more time to pull himself together before the day ahead.

Evelyn rapped on the door three sharp times, took a step back, and gave her hair a quick zhoozh with her fingertips. Don smiled when he held the door open. His arm ushered her through like a man from yesteryear, and her chest puffed itself out a little as she walked through to the kitchen. When she sat at the kitchen bench, she slumped inside and out. But not for long. Her chest opened and out it all came.

She rambled about June taking speed for fun; *for fun*, she repeated numerous times. Don's face didn't show the expected outrage and her voice became more and more shrill as she recapped all the things June had done. And that was only recently, she said, drawing the 'eee' out until she had to take some short sharp catch-up breaths.

'Imagine how long this has been going on for,' she said desperately as her hands became fists.

Although Don hadn't been as outraged as she'd hoped, he mumbled agreeing groans and clicked his tongue as required. She explained how difficult the three days and three nights had been for young Ben and how she had to train June in the laundromat so she could put food on the table and be kept busy, which was the cure to all ills. At this point Don smiled warmly across the kitchen.

'What are you smiling about? There's nothing here to smile about!' Evelyn was incredulous. Don pointed out that there was much to smile about, most of all how wonderful Evelyn was for being so helpful. This stopped Evelyn's runaway feelings and she took a moment to congratulate herself. After all, she was helpful, and she shone inside and out at his pinpoint accurate assessment. This brief pause gave Don a window.

'She loves painting, why don't we bring her over here and set up a space for her to paint? So she has an outlet,' Don said in a low, neutral tone. He stood up and took Evelyn into a lean-to sunroom off the back of the house. Evelyn hadn't noticed it before, but she hadn't really had a comprehensive tour, come to think of it. She had stuck to the lounge, the kitchen, the bathroom and the backyard, which were all on the left side of the house. Once she had peeked into an ajar door, the first on the right upon entry, and had seen a bed with a crocheted coverlet on it. She had assumed it was his bedroom, even though the coverlet had been an unusual choice for a man.

On the way to the sunroom, Evelyn spied two more closed doors but didn't ask about them. After all, she had good manners. The sunroom was small but would be lit from all sides in the daylight. A painting room, she thought to herself. Then a little resentment made its way up to the back of her nose. There she had been with Ben sleeping in a sheet tent in her meagre living room with June on the foldout sofa, which limited her space to her bedroom. And here was Don, all on his own in a sprawling double-fronted house. It didn't seem fair.

When they got back to the kitchen, she flopped back down on her stool and sighed. She didn't want June to go back to her flat. Surely it would give her free reign to 'have fun'. They arranged that June would go over to Don's later that day, after her morning hours in the laundromat, to be shown her creative space. Evelyn swallowed her resentment, thanked Don for joining her in operation 'Keep June busy' and set off home. She had forgotten how annoyed she had been at Don's intervention at first. She hadn't wanted a solution, she had wanted an ear and an ear only, but that was in the forgotten past as she realised her dream of a family was now one step closer from a mere folly.

PART THREE

CHAPTER TWENTY-SEVEN

*E*velyn went to the costume shop two suburbs away and went straight to the counter. She knew what she wanted. It's not that she didn't trust June to perform laundromat duties (she had been reliable for some weeks now), but she felt compelled to see how she behaved unsupervised. Three, or possibly four lifetimes ago, she ran the back bar of a rural hotel and the owner had hovered over her regularly, unpredictably and without notice. Evelyn had been most offended when he had told her that everyone steals to some degree, and it was his responsibility to make sure she was one of the ones who stole the least. When she had expressed outrage at this slur on her impeccable character, he mentioned she had two coffees at the start of each shift, and she had never paid for them. Nor had he ever extended an offer for her to help herself, even though he would have had she asked. Evelyn had agreed that she was, indeed, a petty thief and the information nugget that everyone steals to some degree had stayed with her since. Although it was more June's customer relations that she doubted, given how naturally rude she was.

Evelyn had never forgotten, however, how offended she had been by the hotel owner's compulsion to monitor her, and she wanted to spare June from similar angst. So, she needed a costume. Then she could watch the laundromat goings-on without detection. June always sensed her when she came down the stairs for whatever reason, no matter how quietly she crept. She'd briefly entertained a whizz-bang camera system, but it seemed a little over the top. The solution had come to her in her sleep the night before. A costume. Then she could busk outside, slightly off-centre to the doorway to prevent attracting June's attention, and watch on in secret.

'Hello, I'm looking for a statue costume please,' Evelyn said in her most amiable tone. The young girl behind the counter tucked her chin in to her neck and raised her eyebrows. Evelyn noted this handy way of asking for more information without words and filed it away for later. It would be perfect to help her extract information out of Ben when he was upset about something or other, as words seemed to make him retreat rather than be more forthcoming. Words were the 'it' in a game of emotional chasey.

'You know, those people who stand like a statue and people put money in their hat just for being still,' Evelyn said with a brisk nod at the end. The woman of no words left her side of the counter and walked towards the back of the shop.

Evelyn followed as instructed and was briefly sidetracked by the rack of clown costumes, all brightly coloured and adorned with bows or differently shaped pom-poms where buttons would normally be. Under the rack were stacks of oversized shoes with bulbous toe ends. The patent red leather ones made Evelyn smile, and she briefly wondered whether a clown act would be preferable. But she doubted she had a clown act inside her. She wasn't in the mood to be overly energetic, and sad clowns belonged on stages, not street corners, so she dismissed the clown idea quick sticks and took a hurried few steps to catch up to the thin graceful woman who wasn't as young as Evelyn had first thought.

The woman waved her hand queen-style at three statue costumes, all displayed on mannequins. Evelyn had always liked the tin man in *The Wizard of Oz* the best, so she was immediately drawn to the crumpled silver suit statue standing forlornly next to a matching silver briefcase. Yes, this was the one. After all, Evelyn was a businesswoman, so it wouldn't be too big a stretch. Subterfuge was more likely to succeed when there were tentacles of truth.

Before long, Evelyn was leaving the store with her bulky costume and a tin of silver face paint. When the thin, graceful, age-undetermined lady said the costume was due back at the same time the next day, no discounts for early returns, Evelyn realised why she was so economical with her words. Each and every word had a natural yodel with an inbuilt otherworldly pitch range. Her voice had surprised Evelyn so much that she had stood and stared for a few awkward moments before taking her leave. Wordlessly.

Evelyn guiltily took up two seats on the bus back home, and throughout the trip she pondered how to get in and out of her costume undetected. In the end, she changed under the tree in the backyard with one eye glued to the back door in case June popped out for some reason. As she walked through the back lane and around to the front of the store, she stopped a few times to stretch out her limbs and do a few shoulder rolls to ease her impending stillness. Her knee was still a little hinky after its collapse during the counting ants night, so she practised a mid-walk pose, which put the majority of her weight on her good leg, before rounding the corner to the main street. Perfect.

Before settling into her stance, she placed the crumpled hat on the footpath so passers-by could show their admiration with their coins. Her face reddened under her now shiny silver face, because she wasn't a real busker. But a busker who didn't busk would be more incongruous than a busker who wasn't an actual busker. She faced her mid-walk pose towards the laundromat doorway and stood as still as a brick.

It only took a few minutes for her to feel the ills of being still. Not just physically. She had allowed for her stiff knee, but she hadn't contemplated that her mind would disintegrate at all. Let alone within mere moments. Without head movements, she couldn't follow up on passing snippets of conversation, and she was too far from the door to hear anything inside the laundromat. All she had was herself. She tried visualising Phillip's train set but was unable to immerse herself in the villages. Then she tried her go-to imaginings, like the hot air balloon, the cricket, strolling along the beach with her arm in Don's, but they provided no traction. No relief.

The last time she had been this still, she had been little. She remembered waiting outside the family lounge room, watching her mother. Little Evelyn always stood quietly for as long as she could, so she could gauge her mum's mood and alter her approach accordingly. It could go so badly so quickly. On the better days, her mother's face would register only a brief moment of disgust on seeing her daughter before she'd pull her face together and pretend to be interested. The memory wasn't pleasant, and the exact sick feeling Little Evelyn used to get in her tummy came straight back. A tear rolled down Evelyn's silver face.

'Why is the statue crying, Mummy?' a passing kid said as he stopped in front of Evelyn. His mother was in a hurry and told him not to be silly, because statues don't cry or get sad because they don't have feelings. Evelyn's mind flicked through famous statues and decided that all statues were inherently sad and bogged down in their stillness. David, the Statue of Liberty, Venus (or was that a painting?), the Fallen Warrior, the Veiled Virgin. All were sad underneath the veneer of dignity or embarrassment at their nakedness. Then a series of Buddhas passed her eyes. He was always happy, and she smiled at the thought of Buddha with his head thrown back with laugh crinkles at the side of his eyes. Maybe it was because he was always sitting comfortably. Perhaps the odd standing Buddha had a stool under his flowing robes which made him so comfortable so he could smile.

When she smiled, she felt her face paint crack. Between the cracks and the tear lines, June may recognise her if she took a close look, so Evelyn resumed her stony-faced position. Cupids flickered past her eyes then, but she supposed they were only smiling to convince the world that love induced joy. The world would implode if that myth was debunked, she surmised. Although, truth be told, Evelyn had to admit she was enjoying her patchwork family. And, in varying ways, she did love them. Even June. Don's kind gestures made her stomach warm, his stupid goofy crooked smile made her insides swell until she felt like she just may vomit, and he delighted in her foibles. She simply adored Ben and admired the way he responded to a world that was kinder to others. June had a wicked sense of humour, when she let it out, and enjoyed life more inherently than Evelyn herself; even if it wasn't as often.

Evelyn let her eyes wander to the clock on the laundromat wall. A whole twelve minutes had passed, and she was none the wiser about June's capabilities. As she looked down to see how much money had been tossed into her hat, Tattoo Man and Ash walked past and entered the laundromat. The traffic behind her prevented her from hearing a single word, but she could see him strutting around and pontificating about something inside the laundromat. Evelyn imagined he was feeling hard done by again, and she was desperate to see how June interacted with him. But it wasn't to be.

The statue idea had been sound, but it had borne no fruit. It was lunchtime, and Evelyn's stomach was rumbling. Just as she decided it was time to leave, she saw Ben skipping down the street towards her. She had completely forgotten school got out early that day and calculated that she didn't have time to pack up and run away. Ben paused to wave goodbye to Bruno's son Sam – they walked to and from school together every day since Ben and June had put down roots above the laundromat with Evelyn (why pay rent when they could all bunk in together?) – then resumed his skipping steps towards her. Evelyn shut her eyes. She stared at the insides of her eyelids, which had more and more falling blurry stars skating across them the harder she closed them, crossed her toes in her big silver shoes and hoped he wouldn't recognise her. When she had stolen a quick glance in the mirror above the back laundry sink, she had barely recognised her fully costumed self. So she was probably safe. Then she took a slow breath in to reduce her stress, as worry emanated off people and drew attention rather than averted it.

'Hi, Evie,' Ben said as she exhaled. Evelyn opened both eyes but didn't move a millimetre. She gave him a wink, a Mona Lisa smile and, as she closed her eyes again, she saw him skip into the laundromat. Evelyn was flummoxed.

She had only ever had one response to being flummoxed, and that was to run. So, she ran. First to the backyard where she changed into her own clothes, then to the bus stop, then to the costume store where she was charged for the lost silver shoe and the forgotten crinkly hat. Evelyn had run out of puff, so she walked the two suburbs back towards the laundromat. Instead of going home, she found herself on Don's porch where she paced and paced and paced some more. When the front door opened, Evelyn jumped in fright.

'Oh, hello, Evelyn,' Don said in a mildly surprised but warm tone. 'I was just going to check the letterbox. Would you like to come in for a drink?'

Evelyn stared through him for a moment and wondered why she was there. But she was glad she was. Glad to the bone. She wasn't sure when she had convinced herself that she didn't need to keep running towards a whole new life to avoid the embarrassment of being a busking statue spy. But she was pleased that she had.

CHAPTER TWENTY-EIGHT

*B*en sat in Evelyn's lounge room and watched her load the pile of things they would need for the day into her backpack. He stood, sat, untied and retied his shoelaces, stood and sat again. Her mental checklist was derailed by his fidgeting, so she tipped out the contents and started again. Ben sighed. Evelyn stopped and looked at him.

'Everyone has foibles, Ben, you need to be patient,' she said too harshly. They were as frustrated as each other. Evelyn reminded herself that she was the adult and told Ben she just wanted to make sure they had everything they needed for their adventure.

'What's a foible?' he asked. 'That's a funny word.'

'It's like a quirk,' she said.

'Quirk. That sounds like an animal noise.' He stood up and flapped his elbows with his fists joined at his chest.

Evelyn let out a snort and began flapping her elbows too, then took mini steps with bent knees.

'Quirk, quirk,' she said loudly. Ben flapped his arms, rotated his shoulders and changed his chant to 'Foible, foible.' The pair shared a good old belly laugh and the atmosphere was reset in its afterglow. Ben controlled his impatience, Evelyn sped up her packing process and before you could say, 'Foible, foible, quirk, quirk,' the pair set off to meet Phillip and catch the Puffing Billy train.

A couple of weeks prior, Don had cleared out the sunroom at the back of his house so June could use it for her art. Evelyn had appreciated the gesture, and revelled in the time June had spent there, as it gave her some breathing room in her limited living quarters. The previous evening, the grown-ups had set Ben up at the coffee table in Don's lounge room to draw, while they went out the back and had a chat about the future. It had been decided that June and Ben would move in with Don, who had much more room than Evelyn did upstairs at the laundromat.

Evelyn, Don and June all believed it was their own idea, which boosted seamlessness and paved the way for self-apportioned blame when the inevitable speed bumps popped up along the way. When they discussed logistics (tomorrow was as good a day as any), it was decided that Don and June would do the moving while Evelyn took Ben out for the day. So he didn't get underfoot.

Then it was time to tell Ben. Not only that he and his mum would be moving into Don's house for now, which was exciting enough, but he, Evelyn and Phillip would be going for an adventure the following day. Ben swung into overexcited and ran around the room until Evelyn asked him to please stop before she got so dizzy that she'd be laid up in bed for a week. He was no less excited the next morning, and Evelyn congratulated him on controlling his emotions as they walked over to Phillip's, who had kindly offered to drive them to the Puffing Billy train.

Evelyn was cautious about going in Phillip's car. It was no secret that he was sporadically scatterbrained, topped with easily distracted. But she couldn't help but smile when they approached the flats. Phillip was standing out the front with a crisp blue-and-white striped train driver cap. He took an identical hat out of his beige suit pocket, which looked a little grubbier than usual, and placed it on Ben's head before holding the car door open for them. Evelyn had never seen his car and was surprised, but not surprised, as she crammed herself into the small blue mini hatchback with white racing stripes. Ben had already catapulted into the back seat. Phillip was much larger than Evelyn, but didn't look at all out of place behind the wheel.

When they finally arrived at the Puffing Billy station, the three of them stood on the platform and absorbed the train. The carriages were the deepest red imaginable and the engine was a dark majestic green, accentuated by shiny brass railings and three perfectly round domes on top. The middle dome was slightly smaller than the others and Evelyn had no idea of their purpose. The whistle and the connector rods sparkled in the sliver of sun that had found its way between some sleepy clouds.

'It doesn't look real. It's like when you dream,' Ben said with ta-da arms. Evelyn and Phillip nodded. The conductor was dressed in full regalia, from a stiff hat to a silver watch chain hanging off his waistcoat. The engine driver wore a faded baggy cap, much like Ben and Phillip's, and stiff blue overalls. The signalman walked up and down the platform with pride. The conductor took in a showy big breath and called out, 'All aboard,' and elongated the 'oar' sound for longer than anyone thought possible. Ben ran up and down the platform and signalled the others over when he found the most desirable carriage.

In the third open air carriage, Ben sat on a windowsill and wedged himself between the two parallel window bars so he could relax his whole body without concern for falling. Evelyn was having quite the surrender day, with chancing Phillip's driving and allowing Ben to sit with his arms and legs dangling over the side of the train. They all breathed in the pungent thick grey smoke that pulsated from the engine's funnel. Together they watched the wild daisies fighting the grass for room alongside the tracks, the elegant light grey trunks of the gum trees, the huge wattle trees proudly sprouting pink cylinders, and the varying greens of the foliage.

The smell of the smoke became sweet as it blended with the smells of eucalyptus and drying grass from last night's rain.

Every now and then Phillip spoke – about things like how the volunteers were all ex-railway men, and how the bull bar at the front of the train was pointed, so if they hit a stray animal it would bounce off to one side thereby avoiding a derailing. He told a story of when he was little, and he and his friends would crawl under cattle grids and watch the trains flying past overhead, just inches from their faces.

After a time, Phillip lay his ear on the sill and closed his eyes. Evelyn followed suit and then Ben climbed down to do the same. Each rhythmic intonation flowed through their bodies and the train opened for them like an industrial city. Every sound had its place and purpose. Evelyn pictured little silver men running around with oil buckets so each emerging crack, fissure and fracture could be instantly healed. When the train slowed, the little men refilled their oil buckets and got back to work as they sped up again.

At Lakeside Station, the trio got out to stretch their legs and eat sandwiches and fruit from Evelyn's backpack. Evelyn told Phillip and Ben about the little men she imagined beavering away out of sight to make their journey as smooth as possible.

'Are you magic, Evie?' Ben asked.

Evelyn just looked at him.

'You see magic, that's all,' he said, looking a little embarrassed.

'Well, that's about the nicest thing anyone has ever said to me, Ben,' she said as she turned away to hide her face. She was a little embarrassed too. When they sat back down to enjoy the return trip, Phillip smiled at her. He mouthed that she did see the magic before turning his attention to the view. When they got back to the first station, Ben ran into the souvenir shop. Evelyn had told him he was allowed to pick out one thing, as a reminder of the day.

'I'll put it in my memory drawer,' he said before walking around the store slowly. There were big glossy picture books, colourful t-shirts, conductor hats with train pictures sewn on the front, pencil cases and pencils with rubbers on the end. He ran toy trains across the floor, tried on a shirt and tested the textas. But nothing was right. In the end he settled on a small, plastic faceless engine driver with his clothes drawn on. Evelyn thought it an odd choice but chose not to comment.

After waving goodbye to Phillip at the flats, Evelyn and Ben cut across the park. Not left to the laundromat, but right to Don's house. Ben held his faceless train driver out in front and silently flew him around like an aeroplane. Evelyn wondered what was going through his head, which made her realise she'd been spending less and less time in her imaginings since June, Don, Ben and Phillip had infiltrated her life. The muscle memory was still there, but when she pictured herself in the hot air balloon, at the cricket, at the beach, none of the images took hold. In fact, they seemed such sad, pathetic little pictures that her face blushed and she brushed them away. Real life had more pull now, and she didn't know how she felt about it. Insecurity flowed through her, and she became so heavy she could hardly put one foot in front of the other. Ben sensed her slowing steps, put his train driver in his pocket and held her hand. Slowly, they walked the rest of the way in their real-life bubbles, gaining wherewithal from the other's touch.

CHAPTER TWENTY-NINE

*E*velyn dropped her backpack on the kitchen floor and headed out the back. Don and June had prepared dinner, and there was an ease between them. For a moment Evelyn wondered why June wasn't as comfortable with her, but she dismissed it quickly. Between her being June's boss and nursing her through the hard times, Don had sailed in rather late with his knight in shining armour offer of accommodation and a safe place for June to rebuild herself.

Before dinner, it was time for a tour of the new, but not new, house. Ben's room was first. The adults stood back, and he smiled and shrunk his shoulders in anticipation before opening the door. His bed was longways under the window with a new dinosaur doona cover. He jumped in the air when he saw it and threw himself on the bed. The doona was dark blue with big open-mouthed dinosaur heads all over it. Not cartoons. Artist impressions. Evelyn thought it quite frightening, and the splashes of red throughout looked like the blood of decapitated humans. When she glanced around, it seemed no one else saw the doona cover horror show, so she swallowed her opinion. By the time the golf ball went down her throat, Ben had sat at his desk, laid back on the bed and sat at his desk again. There was nothing new other than the doona cover, but he was as excited as if everything had been handpicked by him and sprinkled with magic fairy dust.

The adults caught his mood and they moved across the hallway to June's room. This was a more subdued unfurling, as she didn't want it to be examined. There was an actual bed base, some drawers and a wardrobe she and Don had found at a local junk shop. The mauve paisley manchester looked peaceful in the dappled light that danced through her window. They'd already all seen the sunroom-cum-art studio, so they headed out the back for dinner.

Ben chatted through the meal about the train, cattle grids and the sounds of the train's insides when you put your ear on the windowsill. He picked up his faceless engine driver, which had sat in front of his plate the whole time, and showed off his new toy. When they'd eaten, Don stood and clinked his glass with a butter knife. It was more of a dull thunk than a ring-a-ding-ding, and he cleared his throat. Evelyn pictured him in an old-fashioned tunic, dirty from saving his olden-day city from marching marauders. A city where everyone knew what was expected of them and felt appreciated for their role in keeping their community intact.

Don explained that June had been working on a surprise for Evelyn, and June rushed off to collect it. Ben smiled beatifically at Evelyn, and she realised they were all in on it. All except her. When Ben went with June, she gained precious alone time. Evelyn loved the quiet but didn't quite understand why she checked her watch from time to time and wondered when they'd be back. June and Ben had been spending more and more time at Don's, making this permanent move there quite logical.

June came back outside with her easel under a sheet, placed it carefully on the grass and made sure it was stable before she revealed her portrait. It was a large black and white charcoal face. Evelyn's face. Not just her outside one. The big open eyes stared at a faraway horizon, while the behind faces looked inwards. It was confronting. A little much. The more Evelyn looked at it, the less she saw her own face. It morphed into a jumble of symbols made up largely of triangles. The cheekbones were greater than and lesser than symbols, the lower eyelids inverted commas. The lips were a twin peak mountain range, the nose became brackets. It was harsh and stark and sad. It caused Evelyn's heart to forget to beat, but not for long.

'I think you've captured my essence beautifully,' Evelyn said as she stood and looked at it from a different angle. June looked mighty pleased with herself, and neither woman noticed the horror on Don and Ben's faces. Evelyn gave a short sharp nod and June rolled it up and tied a red ribbon around it. She presented it to Evelyn who took it as graciously as a queen being given the key to Don's olden day city.

By the time she sat back down, Ben and Don's faces had returned to almost normal.

'So, you really like it, Evie?' Ben asked as he shoved a crust into his mouth. Evelyn noted his tone was drizzled with trepidation.

'I actually do, Ben,' she said warmly. She threw a smile to Don, who also looked a little sceptical. She added a nod to accentuate her honesty and as a sign for him to pull his head in. So June didn't pick up on his doubt.

Evelyn declined sweets, even though tinned peaches and cream was her favourite, and went home. When she rounded the corner, she looked back and waved at the three still standing out front to see her off. It had the air of a momentous occasion, and she felt a little melancholic as she cut through the park on the way home. It was unusual to see no one, and she moved her head around to find someone, anyone, in the wasteland. It was probably how the astronauts felt when they walked on the moon, she surmised, as she slowed her steps to let the isolation seep into her skin.

When she got home, she unrolled the portrait and lay it on the bed. She still saw symbols, but she clearly saw her face sitting behind them, battling its way through to the surface. Her night was filled with elusive chasing dreams – from not being able to find the exit in a sprawling ever-growing house, to her running with a beating heart from a tsunami forming fast behind her. Eventually the wave picked her up by the ankle, like she was as light as a dust particle, and hurled her into the air. She woke at this point, sipped some water and slowed her heart. When she lay back down, she couldn't distract her mind from the ever-growing house that wouldn't let her out and the tsunami that wanted to break her. She redreamed them over and over again with slightly different plot twists until the dawn light faced off and battled the dreams on her behalf; and won. Evelyn opened her leaden eyelids a few times then left them closed with the warm glow of morning de-creasing her face.

CHAPTER THIRTY

*D*on didn't say anything when he held the back door open so Evelyn could put her three bags in the back seat of his car. There was a moment of surprise on his face when he pulled up, but it morphed into a smile so quickly that Evelyn almost missed it. Besides, her mind was busy clicking through her list of all the things she needed for a day trip to the beach.

Since June had become competent at running the laundromat without her, Evelyn had embraced having time to do things and go places. Things she had thought about while she had ironed. Fussing about the laundromat had always given her time to imagine all the things she would do if she had any time, but no time to do them, so she revelled in this unexpected sweet spot. Although real expeditions never lived up to her imagined ones, she charged at each new adventure with a clean slate and an oversupply of hope.

Evelyn took charge of setting the mood for the day by producing a well thought-out playlist for the long drive through the city, the fields, the trees and the meandering narrow roads down to the beach. It kicked off with some jolly 1950s rockabilly tunes. They both smiled at the road while they bobbed their heads separately together.

There was an abundance of hay bales sunning themselves in the fields and Evelyn wondered whether they were always there, or whether they had become more obvious to her after making replicas for Phillip's train village. She supposed that was the way of it. Noticing things for the first time, that were always there, inevitably provided a spate of them. The cows milled about in packs, and she was delighted when she saw eighteen out of twenty-two cows sitting down. Don didn't mind the odd stop to take in Evelyn's moments and, before they were ready, they were there.

Evelyn went to the back of the car, took out the biggest bag and removed a large pair of black gumboots and a pillow. Don slung his towel over his shoulder, put on his sensible legionnaire's hat and waited while Evelyn put on her gumboots, and filled the space between the boots and her legs with a variety of odd socks she had amassed at the laundromat. Her customers had two weeks exactly to ask for missing clothing, after that all bets were off and possession was ten-tenths of the law. Errant socks were plentiful and rarely followed up.

Evelyn had walked over to Don's the previous evening and sat on the new swing seat he had put on his front verandah. He had bought the seat after watching her pace up and down all those times – so she had a comfortable place to battle herself. It had been there for a few weeks now, and Evelyn had never commented on it. But she sure had enjoyed sitting on it and watching the goings-on in the street through the overhanging branches of the magnolia tree in the front yard. Sometimes she sat there with no intention of going inside.

This time, after humming a country and western song about a man who was so blue he had beer for breakfast, she had wandered over to the front door and rapped on it three sharp times as always.

'Shall we go to the beach tomorrow? Just us?' Evelyn had said when he opened the door. 'I'm feeling spontaneous.'

'Who wouldn't want to?' he had said kindly.

'Well, I'm not much for sand, salt water or the sun, but I do so love the beach.' She had stood there waiting for a response and got a little prickly after a few seconds. The man was just standing there staring at her. He pulled himself together and a time was set.

When her gumboots had a rather precise meniscus of socks around the top, she threw her towel over her shoulder, shoved the pillow under her arm and marched down through the sand. Her shapeless red dress billowed in the wind as she lifted her knees up high with every step. She clomped her way through the haphazard strewn bodies to where the dry sand meets the wet, then took three precise steps backwards and lay out her towel. Don followed suit. She fluffed out her pillow, put it at the road end of her towel and faceplanted herself. As the sun warmed her back, she knew she would be asleep too quickly. Don chose to lie face up and turned his too-tight legionnaire's hat backwards so the neck flap created a glowing blue face furnace. This left him wide open for sleep too.

Evelyn revelled in the fall through the earth and let sleep tentacles wrap around her as slowly as possible. These ones had octopus suckers on them, and they de-suckered and re-suckered millimetre by millimetre around her body deliciously slowly. The sounds of children splashing about, and the slapping of upended buckets filled with sloppy wet sand was dreamy white noise. Evelyn loved a crowded beach, squeaky footsteps and sand particles flying around hither and zither as people shook out their towels.

As Evelyn fell down to the depths, Don was rising and floating with the butterflies. Their little fingers had slowly and stealthily made their way towards each other without alerting their owners until they had wound each other up in a pinky promise.

Evelyn didn't know what had brought her back to real life, but all of a sudden she was back. She sat up so quickly, she hadn't noticed where her little finger had been. But she found herself strangely recharged, refreshed, new. The heat from her little finger dissipated when she shook out her hand. The still harbour water that was smattered with boats was only a short walk away, and she decided to leave Don to his nap and go for a stroll. When she looked down at her gumboots, she decided this just might be the day where she let sand near her feet. She took off her boots, placed all the odd socks in a ziplock bag and walked barefoot through the sand. The granules oozed through her toes, and she almost enjoyed it.

When she got down to the harbourside, there was a small platform that seemed to have no purpose. She sat on its corner and placed her feet on the railway sleeper that ran along its side. It was probably there to stop the boats hitting the edge; so their hulls weren't ripped open and their innards exposed to the world in a chorus of shrieking metal before they sunk. Evelyn felt her insides were already ripped open for all the world to see, and she wished she had a railway sleeper too.

There was a growing excited group of frocked-up ladies waiting to go on a larger boat on the bigger platform that had a purpose, and Evelyn watched them bask in their impending celebration through two thick wooden poles with sharpened pencil-top ends. The sun was at its highest and she turned her attention to the bobbing light diamonds on the water at her feet. An absolute desire to fall forward washed through her. She saw herself rolling around like a tumbleweed as she sank, leaving only a ziplock bag of odd socks to show that she had even been there in the first place.

Evelyn pushed her shoulder blades out as wide as they could go and imagined a big red button right in the middle of her back that said 'push me'. Perhaps it would call out to a passer-by who couldn't resist pushing buttons or following instructions. Little Evelyn had pushed each button in all the lifts; so did Big Evelyn when no one was watching. Recently she had seen a big button on the side of a bus stop and had immediately pushed it without thought. It was an ad for a spray bottle filled with an elixir to stop old age, and she had not been pleased when a large dose of mist had smacked her in the face the moment she had pressed the button.

The feeling that she didn't want to exist anymore was over-taken by her increasingly itchy feet. She turned her attention to removing every granule of sand, no matter how steadfast. She hadn't brought her boots, so she doubled up on odd socks and headed back to the wave beach. Don wasn't there, so she stuck her knees up under her chin, waited and watched the swimmers. Don's bright blue legionnaire's hat bobbed up and down as he duck-dived under each wave. When he tired, he slapped his way back up to base. He wrapped his towel around himself, and they both had a little sit together.

'They make a good fish and chips over there,' Don said after not too long and not too short. 'Shall we?'

Evelyn picked up her pillow and gumboots and they traipsed across the sand, him barefoot and her in her doubled-up odd socks.

CHAPTER THIRTY-ONE

*E*velyn had settled back into her old lifestyle at the laundromat, but it had lost a little shine. She would never admit it, but she missed having June and Ben around.

On this night, she closed up shop and headed over to Don's – well, Don, June and Ben's, she supposed. She was pleased that Ben and June had settled in so well, but she was beginning to feel out of place when she visited. The nights when she and Don drank wine, listened to music, sang to his dreadful banjo playing or danced in the square of carpet between the couch and her chair seemed a long time ago. The dinners were still lovely, but she was no longer the glue. They were stuck together, and she was floating around their bond like an astronaut flailing above the mothership. As she cut through the park, she admonished herself for being jealous. That was hard to admit, she thought as she placed her forehead on the same tree that she had used to help keep her brain in on the counting ants night.

There was nothing to complain about. She had achieved exactly what she had wished for. In the beginning she had felt part of the patchwork family, but now she didn't. Not quite. No one was doing anything wrong, and they always made her feel welcome and a part of things, but there was an invisible chasm it seemed only she could see.

When she walked inside, she could hear the three of them out the back. It was a chilly evening, but the cold hadn't been enough to move proceedings indoors. Evelyn thought about popping outside to say hello, but instead she sat on her chair in the lounge room.

'Hello, Evie,' Ben said as he walked into the lounge room. 'Are you coming outside with us?' He took a step towards her but decided against two. Scouting the lie of the land.

'I'm just having a wee sit, Ben, I'll be out soon,' she said with a smile that she forced to her eyes. She knew she was sulking, but she was having trouble taking back the reins.

'Oh, maybe you're having a moment,' he said. He moved closer and put his hand in hers. She smiled genuinely at him, gave his fingers a light squeeze, then nodded. 'Dinner's not ready, yet, I'll get my drawing stuff and sit with you,' he said as he skedaddled out the door.

'What should I draw?' he asked a few moments later, as he lay out his paper and pencils. Evelyn didn't like this dance. She knew that whatever she suggested, he would shake his head, proffer a meaningless reason why her suggestion wasn't the right one, and wait for another option which would also be dismissed. But the dance was the dance.

'What about the cat?' she said with barely enough enthusiasm.

'Nuh, I always draw him.'

'What about an old lady?' she asked. She knew he would have preferred offers of objects rather than people, but she was feeling petulant and closed her eyes.

'Nuh,' he said and waited for more.

Evelyn didn't offer anything else. Partly because she couldn't be bothered, and partly because her closed eyes became immediately heavy and lured by sleep. She thought how terrible it must be to be an insomniac, then mused that they had no idea how annoying it was to drop off anywhere. People who slept at the drop of a hat never spoke out loud about their affliction to insomniacs. Evelyn supposed it seemed so slight an issue in comparison, like when thin people who felt too thin never mentioned it to big people who thought they were too big. Then she stopped thinking altogether and drifted off.

When she woke up, there was a small moment of confusion. She'd forgotten where she was and looked around quickly to establish her whereabouts. It didn't take long to orient herself, and she breathed a sigh of relief. Ben was still sitting at the coffee table drawing away. He had taken some paper, folded a few sheets together to make a book and was at the tail end of the pages. She must have been asleep for a while.

'Hello, darling, looks like you've been busy?' she said kindly. Her jealousy had dissipated during her nap. Ben explained he had waited for her to wake up so she had someone to eat with, because his mum and Don had already had their dinner. He stood up, unaffected by being cross-legged, took her by the hand and together they went out back. Don went straight to the oven and retrieved the pizza slices he had kept warm for them while June spooned out some wilted salad on their plates. The sky was dark, and a few stars shone through the city haze.

Evelyn wrapped her scarf tightly around her neck and shivered. She had tried to suppress it, but Don noticed. After he laid down the pizza he whipped inside and came out with a blanket. He shook it out, not too close, then brought it over to Evelyn. She leaned back in her creaky plastic chair, and he placed it over her lap. The gentle gesture tightened her stomach so much it reduced her appetite. But she had to eat regardless. After all, so much effort had been put into keeping her dinner warm, and Ben had waited for her to wake up.

After a few mouthfuls, she began to enjoy not just the food, but the roundup of what had been happening in their lives. June was working on a portrait of Cheryl (she had such inquisitive eyes), Don had begun late shifts at the paint store so he could take Ben to school while June opened the laundromat, and Ben was enjoying soccer way more now that he was friends with Bruno's son Sam, who had taught him how to foot stall. Ben stood up and put the ball between his foot and his shin and lifted his leg. He could balance it for nearly ten seconds now, and Evelyn clapped.

After she'd eaten, she said she was going to sit inside for a minute and let her food go down. She declined the offer to play Comic Families and Ben was visibly disappointed but didn't say anything. Evelyn appreciated this. She just wanted to leave them to it, really. They obviously had routines now, and there was an ease among them that she was happy to see. She no longer felt slighted that they had melded as a family.

Back in the lounge room, she picked up the book Ben had nearly finished while she'd been asleep. The front cover showed an old lady leaning on a walking stick with one hand and holding a cat in the other. One of the cat's eyes was nearly closed over, just like Don's cat, and she smiled to herself. It was quite the likeness, and she appreciated how well he drew. His handwriting had improved too. The story was about a cat trying to make friends with an old lady. The cat went to extraordinary lengths to get her attention. When he brought her a mouse he had caught, he was surprised when the old lady yelled when she saw it, instead of wanting to pat him. Then the cat caught a bird and couldn't understand why the old lady screamed again, instead of giving him a cuddle. Then the cat jumped up and grabbed the hanging toilet paper and walked through the house with a long streamer behind him. Surely this would make her love him. It did not. And the lady on that page had a very angry face. Then there were two blank pages. Evelyn flicked over to the last page, just in case, and there was the old lady holding the cat underneath the words 'And that's how the cat and the old lady became friends forever'.

Evelyn wondered if she was the old lady. God knows, she had never once shown any inclination to pat or even look lovingly at Don's cat. She did not like it, nor had she realised that perhaps she should have pretended to. Evelyn placed the book as accurately as she could back on the table, so Ben didn't think she was a snoop. She would wait until he had moved onto something else before she stole it.

Evelyn decided that things were best the way they were. Kids were so sensitive to all the facial expressions and actions of grown-ups. There were so many dances she couldn't keep up. She had to encourage the smallest of things, smile when she didn't feel like it, avoid saying what she thought, redo things properly after being 'helped', pretend she was fine when she wasn't. Don was much better at these things than Evelyn, and she let out a short gust of breath through her nose. It was an almost laugh, and it cheered her up. She had an idea and marched herself outside to the others.

Evelyn walked outside with such purpose that the group stopped what they were doing and sat to attention. She asked June whether she'd be a dear and cover her fully at the laundromat for a few days, as she hadn't been away for a while. Don, June and Ben thought this was a lovely idea and all three of them asked where she was going to go at the same time, then laughed at their synchronicity. Well, Evelyn hadn't thought that far ahead and said so, but she would be off the following morning at the crack of dawn. Although she didn't know where she would go yet, she knew that it would be to a mountain town that wasn't too far from the beach. She wasn't planning on starting another new life, but if she did, she sure would love to live in a mountain town not too far from a beach.

CHAPTER THIRTY-TWO

*E*velyn felt light as she walked over to Don's for Sunday lunch. As much as she loved the beach, her days meandering among dancing light spots under the canopies of tall, fat trees had rejuvenated her. It would be difficult to choose from the small scattered villages, and she could see herself with a chestnut cart at one of the Sunday markets. Not that she liked chestnuts herself. The texture reminded her of Spakfilla.

As refreshing as her break had been, she sure was looking forward to seeing her ragtag patchwork family. When she was a few houses away from Don's, she saw Ben standing out the front on the footpath. He was wearing a collared shirt, and Evelyn became immediately suspicious. When she got to the front gate and looked up, there were Don and June holding up a 'Welcome Home Evelyn' sign.

'What on earth would possess you?' she said, marching through the banner with no regard. She ignored the sound of ripping paper, walked straight through to the bathroom and locked the door. She sat on the toilet and raked her fingers through her hair and over her scalp, her nails dug deeper and deeper into her skin with each stroke. 'Fuck, fuck, fuck,' she muttered to herself. 'What is wrong with you?' she said through gritted teeth. Her hands were shaking, and she was sweating from her palms to the soles of her feet.

As she sat there waiting to equalise, she imagined the three of them sitting at the back table planning the surprise. Her surprise. Her welcome home. She knew there would have been some debate about whether they should or shouldn't, and she knew that they would have known they shouldn't, yet they had done it anyway. It was a constant consternation for Evelyn that people did things for themselves under the guise of doing it for others. Friends convincing each other to buy clothes the wearer knew they'd never wear, families arranging funerals they knew the dead would despise, parents dragging children to activities they had no interest in, lovers eating anniversary dinners where they should instead of where they wanted to, partners sitting on couches they found uncomfortable and watching movies they had no inclination to watch. It was endless and audible in conversation snippets everywhere she walked. Dogs, kids, partners being dragged around to unwanted destinations under the blanket of compromise.

Perhaps it was time to leave. To start again ... Again. When she meandered through the mountains, as pretty as it had been, she had vacillated between a new beginning and firmly planted roots with her new family. And as she had walked towards Don's house, sticking around had been so tantalising. But she pushed the temptation away as she sat on the toilet with a now raw scalp.

Seventeen deep breaths later, she went out to face the music. It was up to her to set the tone, and she chose the 'act as though nothing had happened' path. She followed the voices to the backyard and saw an array of snacks on paper plates on the table that should have been thrown out years ago. Right at the centre of the table was a bunch of flowers. She didn't know what they were, but they were plentiful and bright. They stood proudly, each craning their necks over a glass vase with a green ribbon tied around its waist. They did her in. She stumbled over to her creaky plastic chair and lowered herself down. By the time she sat, she could barely breathe. She forced air into her lungs, struck herself on the forehead a few times and a couple of errant tears fell out without a cry behind them.

'Are you okay, Evie?' Ben asked as he slowly approached her from the side. She watched him sidle up with the same caution she had seen him use to approach his mum when she was unpredictable, which was less and less these days. Her own lack of grace turned into vomit which crept up the back of her throat. She swallowed. It was like sucking back a beach ball, and she tried to keep the pain of it from her face. Evelyn tried to pull herself together. It wouldn't do to have the child be afraid of her too. She put on her best warm face, reached out an arm and he fell into her chest. She stroked his hair and muttered, 'Thank you,' a few times. Then she pulled him away from her and looked him squarely in the eyes.

'The sign you made was beautiful, Ben. I'm sorry I ripped it. I just got a fright and my manners fell out.' It was inadequate, but it was the best she could do.

'That's okay, Evie,' he said before telling her all about how they'd had a meeting and written a big list of all the things she liked before going to Phillip's house and inviting him too. The words were too fast, and Evelyn felt dizzy. Her bursts of guilt at her visceral reaction to this lovely, thoughtful surprise party and her love for the boy set off sludge party poppers in her chest.

Meanwhile, Don and June fussed about the table and removed the glad wrap from the party snacks. They had the grace not to mention Evelyn's tantrum, which made her feel all the worse. Evelyn tried and tried to say thank you for the effort they had gone too but the words kept getting stuck behind a lifetime of mud in her throat.

The group settled into reliable small talk. June's word count was higher than anyone had ever heard as she rattled off tales of laundromat customers who had come through while Evelyn had been away. When Phillip arrived, things had settled somewhat, and Evelyn stood to give him a hug. Neither of them were natural huggers. Their first one had been at the completion of laying out the hay bales they had made together, and it had surprised them both. It had been a little awkward as they had both gone to put their heads on the same side, then both gone to put their heads on the other side. Then they had both gripped each other's elbows and nodded, which made them laugh down to their toes. Ever since, they had greeted each other with simultaneous elbow squeezes and entwined forearms as they looked at each other warmly. Evelyn had never seen a *Star Trek* episode, but she imagined their greeting wouldn't be out of place in an alternative universe.

The adults got tipsy, which gave them more energy to kick the soccer ball with Ben. Evelyn even kept goal for a time as the group took it in turns to try and kick it past her through the wooden broom handles covered in tin foil. Three times Don moved the posts a little further apart to give them a better chance.

'Who knew I had the reflexes of a ninja?' Evelyn asked as she stopped the ball yet again. No one scored while she kept goal, and she decided to quit while she was ahead and leave them to it. As she sat back in her creaky plastic chair, watching Phillip try to stop the ball – he didn't stand a chance because his limbs were soggy spaghetti strands waggling around – she felt relaxed. There wasn't anywhere she'd rather be.

Dusk began to show itself and they sat back around the table. Ben asked whether they could play a game of Monopoly, and all their hearts dropped. No one had the energy or inclination. June said it was time to get ready for school the next day. Ben's heart dropped further than the adults' had, and he slumped in his chair. Evelyn remembered being his age and the devastation she had felt each time her parents had declined an invitation to play, to read, to walk, to go out. It had taken so much time and worry to muster the courage to even ask, which made the 'Not now', 'Maybe later', 'Can't you see I'm busy?' responses cut deeper than words should. The memories and relived feelings were not, however, enough to inspire her to join him in a game. If anything, they created a warm forgiveness in the depths of her past. Her parents' complete disinterest in her (everything to do with her had been an enormous chore) had never left her, so this brief spurt of forgiveness was a welcome relief.

Phillip raised a glass, thanked the hosts for putting on such a fine affair, pushed his hat firmly down on his head and left. Don, as always, mustered and suggested to Ben that they start a two-player game. They would go around the board seven times each and then leave the rest for another day. Ben asked for ten times around, please Don, and Don said yes because of his very good manners. Evelyn felt her eyes fill again and poured the last of her wine into her glass. She raised it to June sitting opposite and swilled it down.

'Thank you for everything, Evelyn,' June said. Her voice was open, genuine, and Evelyn let her tears fall without care. She stood and ushered the younger woman over with her hands. Other than the group hug after the zoo, the two women hadn't touched. Except perhaps the odd wash of June's forehead during the three days and three nights when June had 'rested her eyes' above the laundromat. They hugged and let their history course through their bodies. The ups, the downs, the tentative steps they had taken towards each other to make sure the life they were building together didn't shatter, the slow steady trust, the backward steps, the forward leaps sped through their minds as they stood there holding each other.

When they separated, they saw Ben and Don standing at the top of the back steps staring at them agape. They all had a laugh before returning their minds to what was next. On her way out, Evelyn picked up the two pieces of her welcome home sign and rolled them up as she walked.

CHAPTER THIRTY-THREE

*T*he afternoon sun shone through the tree canopy. Evelyn closed her eyes and let the light spots flitter across her face. The back of her head rested uncomfortably on the back of her squeaky plastic chair in Don's backyard, but she didn't want to move. The discomfort was the only reminder she was alive – otherwise she felt as close to transcendental as she ever had. She made sure to only enjoy it for a minute or two. Relaxation had always bordered on intolerable, and this was neither the time nor the place to dwell in her burgeoning imaginings. Young Ben's voice drifted through her reverie.

'Hey, Evie,' he called out lovingly from the back porch before running down the three steps to give her a hug. Evelyn tensed, pulled away and gave him an awkward pat on the back. Don was standing over at the barbeque in a garish red apron with cartoon onions leaping off it. It was a ludicrous apron, and Evelyn wondered who on earth invented the design thinking it would sell, and who the hell else, other than Don, would purchase it. It was bewildering and she looked away to minimise the offence that bubbled away in her belly. Being hungry didn't help. June flopped herself into a nearby chair.

'You look good,' Evelyn said in genuine surprise. June smiled, and Evelyn leaned over and gave her arm a rub. June's spots were gone, her skin was a healthy pink and her hair seemed to have more lustre. It had been a hell of a ride, and both women sat there looking at each other, knowing that the other was thinking the exact same thing.

'What would you like, madam?' Ben said as he stood near Evelyn with a tea towel over his forearm. For a moment Evelyn could picture him waiting in a top-class restaurant with his easy smile and his sad eyes.

'Two sausages, please,' Evelyn said. Ben raced over to Don who let him use the tongs himself. He carefully placed two sausages on a paper plate and called Evelyn over to the salad buffet. Before long, they were all sitting around the table that should have been thrown out years ago. In between firsts and seconds, Don stood up and suggested they raise their glasses, 'To Ben, for getting the most effort award in maths.' They muttered encouraging noises as they clinked glasses, then he proposed another toast, 'To June's full-time job in the laundromat.' Instead of getting seconds, Evelyn let her body fall into the chair. Her mind wandered to the full backpack she had plonked on Don's kitchen floor.

She had emptied her drawer of things past into the backpack that day. She had taken a chisel out of the toolbox and removed the raised metal Whirlpool label off the vintage machine out the back of the laundromat and added it to her bag. The sharp end was placed in the baby bootie, so it didn't scratch anything. She had decided against the ripped 'Welcome home Evelyn' sign, but couldn't resist the stolen book Ben had made about the cat who tried to befriend the cantankerous old woman. Of all her lives, this was the one that deserved two mementos.

Evelyn reflected on her time here, the community she had grown to love. She thought about the nice man with his dog, the frazzled coffee shop couple, horrible Tattoo Man and his lovely girlfriend who seemed destined to tread water for the rest of her life. Cheryl the baker, the new couple at the fish and chip shop who were as zesty as their generously sliced fresh lemon wedges. They would never become bitter like the couple at the coffee stand. Evelyn shook her head when the mismatched family around her asked if she wanted to join in a game of cards.

'Not yet,' she muttered through her fog. The old deck of cards had come from her drawer of things past some time back, and it was a favourite among the group – Evelyn had only lost three times. Her mind drifted back to her bench in the park, the apartment blocks, the two girls, so disappointed by the actions of the 'friend' they had tried so hard to find until they spotted the betrayal. Phillip standing over the saucepan on the sink in his grubby suit. His train set. The tenderness he had shown Ben as he explained the mechanics of it. He was happy the way he was, and Evelyn supposed that she was pretty happy too.

June had found a way through, for now, and the laundromat would keep her on the straight and narrow for a while. Evelyn opened her eyes a fraction and looked at June. She gave her a forty–sixty chance of making the year before falling back into poor choices. There was deep pain, and the girl wasn't naturally happy. Evelyn hoped she would grow to enjoy her son even more than she had so far. At least she knew that Don was in for life. The friend who never lets go. He would watch over them and pick up the reins if June fell off the cliff. Evelyn knew this to her bones; Ben was the son he never had. And they would all miss her. For a while.

Evelyn had left an envelope upstairs at the laundromat for June. It had all the keys, the list of phone numbers for the various repair people and the landlord, who she had worded up about her impending absence. She had taken him for coffee and explained that family business would take her away for some months, and that June would run the business. She had paid four months' rent up front as a buffer and told June in the note that it was due on the thirteenth of each month, no matter what. All the receipt books and paraphernalia associated with taxes and rates and bills were neatly labelled and stacked on the coffee table. It had taken her a week to get it all together, with an instruction sheet on how to keep the accounts, and the phone number of her now ex-accountant.

'Right, Comic Families anyone?' Evelyn asked when the group faded a little. They nodded enthusiastically, cleared the table and the cards were dealt.

Evelyn was torn over the cards. She wanted to leave them right there on the table so Ben would have something to remember her by. The beginning of his drawer of things past. But she had been carting them around with her lovingly since she was younger than he was, and the idea of leaving them behind ripped her chest open. The decision was made for her after the game when she saw Ben turn all the cards the right way up, group them in families and very carefully put them back into the ziplock bag they lived in. It was time to let them go. It also validated her choice of two items from this life, as she now lost one from another.

Evelyn said she needed to pee like Seabiscuit and excused herself. The trio behind her laughed every time she said it, with the same liveliness as the first time. History is a growing pile of little things, and her stomach tightened as she walked inside the house and shut the back door. All the muscles behind her eyes, nose, mouth, chin, face scrunched themselves up tight and tears silently ran down her face. Little foghorn squalls forced their way out of her face from time to time despite her best efforts to keep them in. She put the backpack on her back and made her way through the house to the front door. Past the banjo sitting proudly on its stand, past the record player and the square of carpet on which she and Don danced, through the front door and down the path to the restored gate with the 1920s latch.

By the time she had walked through the gate, she had pulled herself together. Each step she took was one step further from love, loss, grief. Walking away was not just physical for Evelyn and she picked up her pace. Her chest freed, she became taller, and the bounce returned to her step within a couple of blocks. By the time she got on the train, the last station was in the distant past. All she could see was the next stop.

PART FOUR

PART FOUR

CHAPTER THIRTY-FOUR

*I*t was Ben who first realised Evelyn wasn't there. He stood in the kitchen and stared at the space where her bag had been. There was something about the bag that he had always liked. It had so many pockets and he had wished for a bag just like it in his size. Each pocket flap was secured to the bag with thick brown leather straps, not fat coloured zips like his backpacks. When she packed her bag before they went exploring, she always took her time making sure all the things were in the correct pockets, and she did up the straps just so. The ritual was usually accompanied by life lessons, which he tolerated as he'd learned the hard way that fidgeting and being disinterested often led to a tipping out of the bag's contents and another check that all items on her list were present and accounted for.

His stomach knew she was gone, but he couldn't absorb the truth.

'Evie's gone,' he said as he raced down the three back stairs to the yard. Don and his mum didn't understand the seriousness of the situation. June said Evelyn was prone to wandering off and that she wouldn't be far away. Besides, she always came back.

'She's probably forgotten something and gone back to the laundromat,' she said dismissively.

'Evie doesn't forget things,' Ben said. It was high pitched and sounded desperate, even to him. Don put his tongs down and accompanied Ben to the kitchen so he could see the spot where the bag had been. Ben pointed at the empty mottled lino in the hope that Don would now understand. Don looked at him tenderly and said they could go to the laundromat to get to the bottom of things. June pocketed her keys and the three of them set off to put Ben's mind at ease.

Ben ran ahead, then ran back, the whole way there. He felt sick and stopped for a minute, leaned over and gripped his knees. They weren't listening to him, they didn't believe him, and it made yuck in his stomach like the time he spilt his soft drink on the carpet and didn't know what to do. He had placed a cushion over the spillage and turned it into a regular spot to sit and do his drawings at the coffee table. The more time that went by, the harder it became to face the music. The cushion was ignored when the adults cleaned up, because they saw it as a Ben spot. When Ben had lifted the cushion a week or so later, the carpet hair had dried out and stuck together. It was a different colour from the rest with no chance of a cure. Ben had finally faced the music, chose Don as his confessor and led him over to show him the ruined spot in the carpet. Ben loved that Don didn't even care.

'These things happen,' he had said before telling Ben that it was always best to deal with a problem when it first reared its head. He gently explained that solutions were more plentiful the earlier the problem was revealed. In his brain, Ben flicked through the many problems he had caused and thought perhaps Don was right. Trouble got bigger the longer he waited every time.

When they got to the laundromat, Ben sat on one of the padded vinyl chairs while the grown-ups went upstairs to find Evelyn. When he thought they were gone for too long, he crept up the stairs to see what was happening. He sat on the floor outside the ajar door to the lounge room, where he had slept in a sheet tent for three days and three nights while his mum had rested her eyes. He peeked through the crack and listened with all his might. He stretched his ears out as far as he could from the inside and caught snippets of words. Don and his mum were passing a piece of paper between each other over and over again, saying something different each time they looked at it.

Ben gathered that Evelyn had given his mum the laundromat (why would she give them such a big present?), Don expressed disappointment that she hadn't had the fucking courage to speak to them in person (Ben had never heard Don say the

F word), they both wondered where the hell she had gone and, at separate times, said there was something inevitable about it. Ben didn't know what inevitable meant before that, but he developed a sense of it as he sat there on the floor.

The insides of his ears contracted, and he stopped caring about anything they said anymore. He wanted to ask if Evie would be back for his birthday, because he was turning nine soon and Evie had told him they would have a double-layered cake in the shape of the number nine. She had told him that the number nine was often overshadowed by the upcoming double digits, and number nine knew itself to be insignificant in comparison. But number nine was actually quite handsome when given due consideration. They had been at the park for this discussion, and had taken some sticks and written the number nine in the dried dirt under the big tree where the grass didn't grow. They erased them with the bottom of their shoes and did it over and over again, and Evelyn had told a story of when she was nine.

Ben often asked her to tell a story about when she was whatever random number he chose. It was one of his favourite games. It was special because they only did it when they were alone together. Evie was forthcoming on every occasion and Ben had learned a lot about his best friend through these stories. It made him see that his path and life had been walked before, and it gave him great comfort. It made him feel less alone.

'When I was nine,' Evelyn had begun in the same upcoming fairy tale tone she used when it was time to settle in for a story. It was always said with grandeur and induced immediate anticipation in his chest. She had told him about all the cool girls who did cartwheels and handstands against trees at lunchtime. The girls who were so far away from Evelyn that she might as well have been in Malta. Ben asked what Malta was and she told him about a country far away on the other side of the world. The smallest country there ever was where people ate rabbit stew and widow's soup. Evelyn had practised handstands after school for many weeks and then one day she stood next to a tree and coughed loudly to get the attention of the girls who did cartwheels and handstands and the kids lolling around half watching them.

Evelyn told Ben how she proceeded to do the biggest, bestest handstand that ever there was, but when her feet went to find the tree trunk to support her, there was nothing there. She had flipped straight over onto her back beside the tree and the laughter that ensued from the girls who did cartwheels and handstands against trees every lunchtime and the kids lolling around half watching them rang in her ears for years to come. She told her mum she was too sick for school the following day and had even rubbed toothpaste on the back of her tongue, because the throat end of the tongue often goes white when you're sick. But her mum had told her to get her bum to school and to stop carrying on.

Surely Evie would be there for his ninth birthday, he thought as he sat at the crack of the lounge room door. He sensed movement, went down the stairs on his bum to prevent footstep noises and resumed position on the padded vinyl chair. When Don and his mum walked into the room, he looked up and saw that Don's face was particularly stricken. It was Ben's new favourite word. Evelyn had told him it was like your feelings had been hit with a stick. This happened a lot to Ben, and he had asked her if it was hereditary because his mum often looked like her feelings had been hit by a stick too. Ben would never forget the look on Evelyn's face when he had asked the hereditary question. Normally her face was like stone, but it had melted like ice-cream on a hot day and all her feelings were there for him to see. She had looked sad and proud and broken, but also solid, all at the same time. And she didn't say any words; instead, she had just pulled him into her arms, which she did more and more often as time went on. They had known each other for the longest time before the first hug, but after that the hugs just kept coming like minutes.

'Let's go home and have a talk,' Don said as he squeezed Ben's shoulder. When June unlocked the door, Ben ran straight out the laundromat's front door and up the street to the park. He threw his head from side to side, hoping to catch a glimpse of Evelyn. He forgot what she was wearing and stopped dead in his tracks while he sucked in deep breaths that were shallow at the same time. He couldn't get enough air but he was choking on so much air that he swallowed and coughed up an air ball. Spit went everywhere but he didn't care, even though it was embarrassing.

Ben heard a large groan and turned to see where it had come from. There was no one there. It had come from him. He fell onto the grass and pounded it with his meagre fists. He had never felt so small. Then he tried to put his thoughts into order. Was she wearing purple? Where was Nutmeg? Why was he thinking of Nutmeg? Where is Evelyn? She wouldn't. Why? Did he do something wrong? Then his memories swirled around the inside of his eyelids, and he saw Phillip's trains chugging around corners, but they weren't Phillip's trains. They were pictures of Evelyn, of his mum, of Don, of the biggest arsehole bully in the world from school. He had no idea why he was seeing the bully, his teacher, the big girl from grade six who walked around the oval at lunchtime taking the same exact steps every day without ever looking up.

When his arms were sore from punching the ground and he couldn't punch anymore, he stood up. He didn't brush any of the dirt off him; he wanted to rub it into himself but didn't know why. The tear lines on his face felt like burnt trenches, but they felt good at the same time, so he didn't rub his face even though it was itchy. Again he looked around. Even though he knew he wouldn't see her, he had to try. Instead of running, he meandered through the streets. His body took him to the petrol station where they had eaten ice-cream. He dusted himself off then went in to ask for the bathroom key.

The man looked around behind him and out the window for an accompanying adult. But Ben didn't have an accompanying adult, and the realisation pulled his shoulders down to the ground. He left without the key but pounded on the toilet door just in case she was in there hiding. She wasn't, and he knew it. It was time to go home.

When Ben rounded the last corner, he saw Don standing in the street. He wasn't looking, he was just waiting. Ben walked over, stood next to him and they both stared at the street together. Presently Don put his hand on Ben's shoulder and gave it a squeeze. Ben liked that Don didn't try to say words because all the words would have been wrong, and they both knew it. Something passed between them, but Ben didn't know what it was. He couldn't catch it, nor did he try.

'When the worst things happen, eating food is like swallowing tennis balls,' Don said, finally breaking the silence. Ben thought that was a very strange thing to say given all that had happened.

'I don't think a tennis ball would fit in my mouth,' Ben said, opening his mouth as wide as it would go. He put his fist into it and bit down on his fingers as hard as he could, even though it hurt. It induced a new round of tears and his chest heaved and hoed like a ship in rough seas. A ship of feelings. Ben imagined a ship going up and down the waves with huge water splashes washing over his brain at each descent and he wished he was better at drawing. He would love to draw that ship. He told Don about the ship of feelings that slowly let all the sad out each time it tumbled down the waves. Don listened without moving. Ben wanted to shake him until answers fell out, then he could pick them up and swallow them whole like big tennis balls until his belly was so full of answers that he wouldn't have to cry anymore.

They turned around at the same time and made their way up the path towards the house. It was a slow walk. The walk towards a life that would never be the same. The walk where the past was left behind them. Ben wondered if Don knew that everything would be different once they walked through the door to a world without Evelyn.

In the moment they paused at the threshold, Don fell to his knees on the front doormat. Yes, Don knew this was the beginning and the end too. Ben put his arm around Don's back, and it hardly reached his other shoulder blade. Ben wondered how Don could ever have been as small as him and whether he could ever be as big as Don, who stood up, turned his back to the door and picked Ben up. They stared at each other, but they were blurry because their faces were so close their eyes couldn't focus properly. Ben could see his mother standing at the end of the hallway near the kitchen door in the background, but he didn't take his eyes off Don. She was blurry too, but he couldn't think about her right then. Unless she ran up the hallway and took him into her arms as well.

But she didn't.

Ben watched her form walk into the kitchen. Her shoulders weren't even down. Ben felt a new stab through his chest. Like a javelin sailing through the air in the Olympics, but instead of landing in the grass and quivering proudly in the air, it went straight through the middle of his chest to somewhere else. He hugged Don as tight as he could. If he never let go, maybe Don would stay forever without ever having to rest his eyes to get away from him.

CHAPTER THIRTY-FIVE

*E*velyn did not come to Ben's ninth birthday party. A part of Ben believed she would. But she didn't.

Don bought three sponge cakes to allow for their inexperience at cutting them into number nine shapes. A good thing too. Don placed the number nine stencil Ben had made on top of the first cake and carefully ran the knife around it. Ben was watching closely, breathing only when he needed to. When the tail of the nine promptly detached itself and toppled over, Don told him not to worry. That's why they had a spare. The second attempt was jagged around the edges, but in one piece, and the third wasn't half bad. Then June whipped the cream with a hand beater, a remnant from Don's childhood. It had a wooden handle up the top, a circular gear turned by a matching wooden teardrop toggle, and two whirly gigs that spun the cream. Ben had been busting for a turn and, as always, it wasn't as fun as it looked. But he kept at it and worked the beater until little hills formed in the cream as instructed.

'They're called peaks, not hills,' June said as Ben made as many hills on the top of the cream as would fit. He called them hills in his mind regardless. June got one of Don's old butter knives that had a flat blade and a bone handle and ran the icing around the double-layered number nine with cream in the middle, and Ben got to lick it clean after he had run his tongue around the beater's whirly bits to get the cream. He knelt on a chair up at the kitchen bench and watched the grown-ups do the dishes. June always dried, even though Don always said she didn't have to because the dishes would dry themselves just by sitting on their own for a while. They had the same banter at the sink each time, and Ben liked the pattern of it.

'Are you sure you don't want to invite anyone from school?' Don asked as he finished up. Ben shook his head. He had thought about it seriously. There were a few kids that would come, but even though the party games Don said they could make sounded fabulous to Ben, he knew the other kids would think it was lame. One kid had recently had a Pokémon party where everyone except Ben had dressed up and gone bowling. His party wouldn't compare and would damage his reputation. This way, they had nothing on him.

No, he was happy to have his mum, Don and Phillip come around, eat a cake and kick the ball around the backyard. It was enough.

When his birthday finally came, Ben woke up early. He knew he would get a present of some sort, and it was nice that his big day fell on a Saturday. He was looking forward to the day ahead. At high noon, the snacks and cake were sitting atop the table that should have been thrown out years ago. They all called it that now, and Ben liked that a table could have a name. He waited inside while the table was being set and when Don called him outside, he was delighted to see three wrapped presents on Evelyn's squeaky plastic chair and a round pigface piñata hanging from a tree. Even Don's straggly white cat with one half-closed eye was lolling around on the grass. The cat often disappeared for days on end and when Ben asked where it went, Don said it was a flirt and probably had five different families that all thought he was their cat.

When Phillip arrived, he was carrying a big oblong box and a foldout square table with thin delicate legs and a green vinyl top. It was old but sturdy, he said as they cleared a corner in Ben's bedroom. The drawers were moved right next to his bed, which would be a great spot for his books, and the table was erected where the drawers had been. Ben sat on the bed and opened the big heavy box. A train set. His very own train set.

Phillip showed him how to connect the tracks, start the engine and turn its lights on for night-time. The pile of small things to start his village was what pulled on Ben's heart the most. Little streetlights, a cabin, some trees and his very own imaginary family. Ben's eyes filled with tears and Phillip carefully avoided looking at him while he was emotional. He was overcome with gratitude as Phillip explained each item from the box, and Phillip's words barely weaved their way in through his thick feelings.

The trio sang 'Happy Birthday' at the top of their lungs, except June who looked a little embarrassed at the volume, then they all ate the food, kicked the ball and admired the new soccer jersey that Don had given Ben. He proudly showed off his sketchpads, brand-new set of pencils and pastels that smelled like oily mud perfume that his mum had given him. The third present, wrapped in a shoebox to hide its identity, was a voucher for the bookshop in the next suburb. Don said he would take him there after school on Monday and he could choose his own books, because he didn't want to get him the wrong ones.

Every now and then throughout the party, Ben would hear something, stop still and push the insides of his ears out to listen for Evelyn while he looked at the back door. When he had said they should leave the front door open in case she came, Don got that sad look on his face for a few moments, which matched the way Ben's stomach felt when he thought about Evelyn. Together they had wedged the front door open with a brick. For just in case.

At the end of the party, Ben sat there looking at the remnants of food on the paper plates with Superman pictures on them and realised, again, that she was gone. He wondered why each realisation was just as painful as the one before. But he didn't cry this time. For a moment he had to push the cry away. He breathed through the sick feeling in his tummy, widened his eyes to stop any stray tears and vowed to never cry for her again.

CHAPTER THIRTY-SIX

*W*hen Ben and his daughter returned to the old house from the cemetery, Ben lowered himself gingerly down into the swing seat that had been languishing on Don's front porch since Evelyn had left. Young Ben had spent some time swinging on it in the months following her departure, but he had sat on it less and less as he slowly adjusted to life without her. There had been a moat around him, a void. Everything was so quiet after she left.

Don took him places, as did his mum on her sporadic trips back to the house, but the adventure and magic were missing. He had, however, been able to picture Evelyn wherever they went. Her wide wondering eyes, the tales she would have inserted on his surroundings and passers-by. It wasn't the same, but it was the same.

The swing seat creaked and squeaked, but it held. He pushed the seat gently with his foot; it reached the floor now, and the seat swung on one side but not the other. His daughter sat on the front step reading her book. Every now and then she turned to look at him in case there was movement. He didn't know why he had been so insistent on her coming with him. Her mother had tried to gently cajole him into going alone, but he had steadfastly held his ground. Now he realised his daughter hadn't really wanted to come, but she hadn't had the heart to say so.

Ben pushed himself up with all of his might and stood for a moment to let the sudden rise settle. A wry smile formed as he thought back on all the times Evelyn got a case of the dizzies. He went to the car and got out the fresh bedding he had packed and headed inside to make up their beds. His daughter followed a few feet behind him the whole time. When he flopped the armful of bedding on the old couch, she let out an 'Oooofff'. He looked down and saw her hand over her mouth, as if to stop any further thought explosions. He followed her gaze and saw the framed portrait his mother had made of Evelyn. Ben had found a corner of the portrait peeking out from behind Don's wardrobe the last time he had been to the house, and had hung it pride of place. Given that Don had chosen to frame it, it seemed fitting that it should finally be on display.

'Who's the scary black and white lady?' she asked. Curiosity trumped silence.

'That's Evelyn,' Ben said softly, 'that's who you're named after.' Evie looked dumbfounded. It brought home how expressionless she was in general. He was torn between wanting to make the beds before the musty couch dust infiltrated their sheets and telling her about Evelyn. Two birds one stone, he thought, as he asked Evie to give him a hand making up the beds.

When they walked into Ben's old room, nothing much had changed since he had left home. The bed was still under the window, although it was a big bed now.

'I haven't slept in a big bed, yet,' Evie said as she tried to tuck in the corner of a sheet. It hadn't crossed his mind that she wouldn't know how and made a mental note to teach her the basics. Just because he had grown up too early didn't mean Evie didn't need to learn life skills. Ben patiently demonstrated hospital corners, just as Don had shown him, and he told Evie about the lovely lady in the laundromat (what's a laundromat?) who used to give him bakery treats (from Baker's Delight?) at the formica table (what's formica?) on Washing Day Tuesdays (but you can do washing on any day).

'It was my favourite day of the week,' Ben said with nostalgia as he shook the doona cover on. He told her when his mum got sick (is that when she died?) they went to live above the laundromat (why didn't the lady have a house?). And how the lovely lady and Poppy Don took him to the zoo (can we go to the zoo, Dad?) and kicked the soccer ball at the park, and how the four of them made a family. All thanks to the lovely lady at the laundromat.

'How come I never met her?' Evie asked. She was sitting on the made bed, tightly hugging her pillow; she looked out of place.

'She left before you were born,' he said matter-of-factly. 'Righto, let's do Poppy Don's bed next.' Ben hadn't factored in how depleted he would feel at explaining his back story and willed away his malaise. The conversation turned to Poppy Don once they got into his room.

'I miss him,' Evie said. Her voice was even smaller than usual. From the moment she was born, Don had been a doting, loving and patient grandfather. Ben had never forgotten the way Don had looked at Evie when she was first born. He had waited so patiently for his turn to hold her, but the man with all the time in the world had been unable to stop his arms from reaching out too quickly when it was finally his turn. Nor could he stop the silent tears that ran down his creased face into the edges of his broad smile. Ben had always known Don's love, but the depth of it had not been apparent until that moment. His wife saw it too and shooed them out of the room.

'Take the baby, I could use a little rest,' she had said, even though they knew it wasn't true.

'I miss him too,' Ben said as he sat next to Evie on the frayed crocheted coverlet that Don never took off his bed, except to give it a shake and a little airing out on the front porch from time to time. Ben realised he had never asked where it had come from. What it stood for.

'I'm a bit scared in that room, Dad,' Evie said. Ben knew it would take some courage for her to sleep in a strange room. And it made sense. These were his memories, not hers.

'Let's make tents out of sheets and sleep in the lounge room,' he said as he stood up excitedly. Even though Evie said she was too old for sheet tents – the pair had spent hours reading books together in makeshift cubbies when she was smaller – she soon developed enthusiasm and made suggestions for a sturdier structure. Their memories flooded the room, and they both giggled each time the mattresses they dragged from the bedrooms fell to the floor on the way through. Their tents resembled four-poster beds fit for princesses in the Taklamakan desert and they set off to the sunroom to find the torches.

June's easels and paintings had been pushed to the far corners many years ago, and were almost hidden by all the boxes, tool chests and household items that were superfluous, yet Don thought too good to throw out. When the torches were unearthed, the pair headed back to the lounge room, turned off the main lights and lay down in their sheet tents.

'I love this tent, Dad, it's really cosy,' Evie said through the sheet wall.

'Me too,' Ben said quietly before closing his eyes. But sleep did not come.

CHAPTER THIRTY-SEVEN

Many years ago, Ben had learned to calm his breath and just lie there when sleep didn't come. For a while he'd let anger and frustration seep through him; sometimes he'd cry, sometimes he'd punch his pillow until he had no fight left in him. But he soon learned the futility of reacting, of feeling, of caring. It started the first time his mum didn't come home. Unlike when they lived at the flat, she didn't even bother leaving a note. Worry kept him an arm's length from sleep for many nights. Until one night he was so defeated, he just lay there letting his mind go around, uphill and down dale until sleep finally came all by itself. Now, as he lay there in the sheet tent beside his daughter, he closed his eyes and waited while his thoughts and memories flitted and danced about freely.

He wondered whether his mother's mind did the same thing when she used to come home and rest her eyes for a few days. Each time June came back, Don would put on a dinner at the table that should have been thrown out years ago, and June would do her best to keep her eyes open before heading off to rest her eyes on the couch, or in bed. She'd come good, integrate back into their daily lives, return to laundromat duties and pick Ben up from school as though she'd never been away in the first place. And then, just as he began to relax and trust her presence, she'd be gone again.

Don was always gentle in managing Ben's expectations of his mother. He would stick up for her, which annoyed Ben, and when he didn't, that annoyed Ben too. Don walked the tight-rope of lose–lose as best he could, and never lost his temper.

The second time June left was when Don made the decision to close the full-service wash and ironing section of the laundromat. It was too much to keep the laundromat operating fully while working in the paint shop, and Ben and Don quickly settled into a routine. They went to the laundromat every morning at five am, no matter what, to clean up and prepare the space for the new day. Bleary-eyed, they'd sweep and mop the floor, fill the coin change machine and make sure the washing powder dispenser machine had enough little packets in it. That was Ben's favourite job. He took great care to ensure each mini detergent box faced the same way and all were perfectly stacked to prevent one getting stuck on its way out of the mystery slide. Evelyn had shown him how to stack the machine one day, and he had delighted in her praise when he made the effort to do it just so. He supposed his organisation and preparation skills began with her.

But Ben never went to the laundromat with June. He steadfastly refused. The first night June had asked him whether he'd like to come and help out after school in the laundromat, Ben had said no rather aggressively. Don said there was no need to be rude to his mother. Ben swallowed his betrayal and went off to sulk in his room after closing the door too firmly. He had cried himself out, and every now and then he sensed someone standing at his door. When he looked down, he saw two meek shoe shadows standing there, shifting from time to time.

'Is someone there?' Ben had asked when he was ready to crawl back to the world.

'Yes,' Don said, then waited for an invitation to come in.

And so began the tradition of how Don and Ben worked through anything that happened. Don would open the door after hearing his invitation and gently take steps across the room, like he was walking across sinking stepping stones. Ben would invariably smile at Don's care-filled ginger approach, and it was only when Ben smiled that Don would take the last steps, turn the desk chair around to face him and shift restlessly until he found a comfy spot. This usually meant one leg sitting across the other and angled so the light from the window would speckle on his face.

Then there was usually a standoff for who would speak first. If Ben didn't, Don would rabbit on about a strange colour someone had chosen at the paint store. He would shake his head and ask why anyone would want to paint a garish orange wall in their kitchen, when it would only be suitable for a fire-breathing dragon. Then he would ask Ben how his latest storybook was going and suggest if ever he wrote one about a dragon, he had just the colour for his illustrations. Ben showed Don all his storybooks, and each birthday, Christmas and on special Sundays, they would go to the bookstore and art supply shop to replenish Ben's supplies.

In the tent, Ben's eyes welled up as he remembered always having more than he needed to feed his storytelling. There was a constant stream of 'You never know when you might need some charcoal' or some such thing when they shopped. Don had been there through thick, thin, ups, downs – always supporting his interests and pastimes. The water in his eyes tipped out and made its way to the edges of his ears. He didn't wipe it away.

Ben's mind tentacled from Don to Evelyn. He couldn't remember her being at his eighth birthday and remembered viscerally that she had left just before his ninth. He flicked through the memories and saw how each had tidal-waved the course of his life. He remembered her refusing to let him retreat into a corner when his mum rested her eyes for three days and nights at the laundromat, how she had drawn him out and made him play Chinese chequers. How Comic Families was the activity that brought the four of them together, the nights out the back, the move to Don's, which in hindsight had been her plan all along. She had built him a safety net of Don. Perhaps she had known his mum would succumb to her pain. The pain he would never know or understand. There were no family members he could ask to find out why his mother was the way she was.

Evelyn may have seen some of herself in June. They were both runners, and she had planted boy Ben with an anchor. A sturdy, loyal, steadfast rock of a man who never gave up on him. Who would never leave him. Ben briefly chastised himself for his previous resentment towards her. She had given him a family. A family of two.

Ben did not, however, have the same grace or gratitude towards his mother. The older he got, the further away she moved from forgiveness. He had told his daughter and anyone who had ever asked that his mother had died. And she had – to him. Who knew where she was, or whether she was even alive. The not knowing had bothered him for a long time. But not anymore.

Ben had been twenty-two when he had last seen his mother. She was standing on the street corner at his favourite pub. When he saw her, he stopped, and they looked at each other for the longest while. She searched his face. He knew if he walked past her, she wouldn't have said a word. She would have just walked away. Again.

'Shall we have a drink?' he had asked. The words hurt his throat like he was spitting rocks. She smiled with trepidation and nodded. They had sat at the bar and waited silently for their drinks to be poured. He paid; she didn't protest. She was so thin. Brittle. If he spoke too loudly, he worried she'd shatter into a thousand pieces. She asked after him, and he filled her in mechanically. He was studying fine arts at university. She gazed at the folio he had been carrying, and he wanted her to ask to see his work.

'Maybe you got your talent from me?' she said. He wasn't sure whether she was trying to inject humour to break the awkwardness.

'Maybe, Mum,' he had said, then paused for a long sip of liquid that hadn't worked as quickly as he'd hoped. 'We've never really spoken about us, about why you leave, have we?' he asked. He hadn't realised how desperately he'd wanted answers, and he patted himself on the back for making the first move. He braced himself for a real and true conversation and tried to grasp questions that sped past his eyes so quickly he could barely see them.

'No, we haven't,' she said. After the smallest of pauses, she stood, parted his hair straight down the middle and kissed the top of his head. He had forgotten how she used to do that. 'Anyway, I'm glad you're doing well, I have to go.'

And that was that. He had been so shocked, he hadn't been able to react. Or even move for a while. A friend passed him at the bar and asked if he wanted to join a group of his friends out the back. Ben shook his head, even though the girl he loved was out there. The girl who knew most of his story. He was pretty sure she liked him too, but it wasn't enough to draw him out of himself. Instead, he headed home and went straight to his room and closed the door a little too firmly. He could see Don's shadow feet on the other side of the door, but he didn't ask if anyone was there. Not that time.

The memory still put a pang in his chest, but now, as he lay there in the house that had given him a home, it was barely a blip. Evelyn and his mum's leavings meant little now. His mother had given him art, Evelyn had given him stories, and Don had given him love and loyalty.

CHAPTER THIRTY-EIGHT

*A*fter a couple of hours, Ben climbed out of his sheet tent and went to his old bedroom. He turned his desk chair and faced the window, much as Don had done over the years when they had their talks. He stared at the small chest of drawers beside his bed. The bottom one hadn't been opened since he'd turned double figures. It was his abandoned memory drawer. And it was time.

When he opened it, his hand rushed for the Comic Families game that had brought the four of them together at the table that should have been thrown out years ago. The illustrations made him smile and gave him as much joy as he had felt when he was small. The truck he had once loved so much didn't bring any spark, so he left it there. The photo, the only picture of all of them together, was precious. Some black spots were feathering their way across the image, blocking out his and Evelyn's cat paintings. Don and June's cat paintings were still visible, and Ben felt warm as he remembered their first ever dinner together. It was so Don, to have planned a group activity to bring them together, and he searched his own face for answers. There were none. He was just a boy, clearly enjoying himself, and Evelyn's hand was squeezing his shoulder. The plastic moulded station master with painted-on clothes brought a smile to his face. There was one more item left in the drawer. He pulled out the first picture book he made after Evelyn had left and slowly flicked through the pages.

It was about a sad whale who didn't understand why some whales left their pod. The sad whale swam and swam as far as he could away from his pod to find the ones who had left. To find a better place. The sad whale travelled so far he got imprisoned by walls of kelp, which made him appreciate what home was. The shaded pencil illustrations were crude, but full of feeling, and the words were disjointed. But the idea was sound. His seventh children's book was being released next month. It would be the last in the series of the lost one-eyed cat who went from place to place in search of home. Its success had surprised Ben, but it was time to put it to bed. He wanted to branch out into less autobiographical stories. To prove his creativity to himself. Deadlines and the task of packing up his home had been used to delay his freedom. After tomorrow, there'd be no more excuses and he felt a little queasy as he shuffled back to the sheet tent.

CHAPTER THIRTY-NINE

*A*lthough Ben was strung out from little and fitful sleep, he stood up with purpose. It was time to let the past go. While Evie made toast (she loved helping), Ben took his backpack with leather straps and stuffed the contents of his memory drawer into its base. He placed a jumper over the top and wondered why he was hiding his memories. And from whom.

The pair sat on the three back steps and ate their toast in the morning sun. He told Evie about his childhood community. After Evelyn had left, they had found an extended family in the neighbourhood. When Poppy Don worked at the paint shop, Ben would go to Cheryl's bakery after school, where he would sweep the path and wipe down the outside tables and be rewarded with snacks. Sometimes he'd go to Bruno's shoe repair shop, where he was allowed to put sticky hot glue on the back of leather pieces with a metal paddle-pop style stick and watch Bruno meld the pieces onto shoe soles. Sometimes he'd skip down to the coffee cart and get a free hot chocolate with two marshmallows from the couple at the coffee cart just before they closed for the day.

Ben told Evie about Bruno's son, Sam, who was coming that morning to help them load the skip. He and Sam used to kick the soccer ball around the park where he and Evie had eaten their fish and chips the day before. Sam was one of the popular kids, and mostly they played when the other kids weren't around. But one day, Sam had put his arm around Ben and told the cool kids that he was too busy to play with them because he had already made plans with Ben. Evie put her head on Ben's shoulder, and he told her that, when they got older, he and Sam would sit on the platform of the climbing frame and talk the night away. Sometimes Cara, Cheryl's daughter, would come too.

Ben looked at his watch and said the others would be arriving soon. The pair set off out the front and looked at the big battered blue skip bin. They began filling it with items they could do by themselves, and when Sam turned up, Ben was delighted to see that he'd escorted his father from the nursing home to say goodbye. Bruno pinched Ben's face so hard it left a red mark, but Ben didn't protest. Love was love. Bruno sat on the old swing seat as the men carried out the couch and two remaining mattresses. Ben called the bakery and placed a coffee order with Cara, who had turned the old bakery into a modern French patisserie, and he and

Evie set off to pick the order up while Sam sat on the front step and kept his father company.

Evie enjoyed her chocolate snail immensely as she didn't often get sugary treats, and after the morning tea the three of them finished loading the bin. As magic hour hit the skies, Ben and Evie waved goodbye to Sam and the old man. When they went inside to the empty house, they opened all the windows to let the light and air fill the rooms. Ben vacuumed the threadbare carpet – the stain from the soft drink was still there – and before dusk set in, the job was done. Evie waited in the car while Ben did one last walkthrough to say goodbye.

Ben slung his backpack with the many pockets and leather straps over his shoulder and locked the door for the final time. He tucked his memory drawer into the footwell of the back seat and turned right out of the driveway; and much like Evelyn all those years ago, he didn't look back.

ACKNOWLEDGEMENTS

*I*t takes a village.

The House for the Temporarily Defeated members sat around the lounge room listening to me rabbit on about the nameless woman who had moved into my head and unpacked her suitcases. When I said she needed a name, their ears pricked up, and they peppered me with questions about her characteristics, what she looked like, what she would do if faced with hypothetical scenarios and many names were bandied about. This discussion led to me getting to know my new leading lady more and more by the minute, and led to the name Evelyn. Thank you, Cailin. Young Hally, who spent many a night playing board games with me, constantly reminded me of Evelyn's essence when I postulated new storylines. Sullivan eagerly awaited new chapters, pushed me along with his natural grace, cried and laughed at Evelyn's adventures and dreams, and I doubt that I would have delivered this book without him. When I told Austen that I was picking a child to dedicate the book to, he said that Sull was my right-hand man and was chuffed for him. Typical Aus – always there with his even disposition and easy smile to brighten our days.

When the draft was finished, I ran it through my early readers – a nervous time. Thanks to Agent Grace for her unwavering belief in Evelyn and for shattering my stumbling blocks along the way; Jonno for saying I make mundane everyday things so interesting (that's going on my resume); Kylie Doyle, who pointed out that she kept waiting for something to happen (me too); Em and my brother Sam, who ran through notes and pointed out induced emotions page by page (perhaps it was as funny-happy-sad as I'd hoped); and to Sandy Weir for being on my side and by my side, especially when I was awash with panic and self-doubt.

Sam got hit by a car the day after I handed in the manuscript. When he emerged into semi-consciousness, most of my hospital visits were spent listening to how saddened he'd been by Evelyn's inability to walk the earth with the other humans, and then how uplifted he was when he realised that our Evelyn was perfectly happy sitting on the moon with only one moonboot all by herself. As he healed and returned to the Sam I'd always known, and then some, with his boosted love for those around him (thanks to The Good Accident), he said that this book was better than the first and that it was high time he took the challenge and lifted his writing game. See you on the dance floor, darling.

Lastly, but not lastly, my more-than-a-publisher Vanessa Radnidge from Hachette, who has shown unwavering belief in me and my writing. When I had wobbly patches, she nursed me through. But it was her difficult conversations, especially 'I don't think you know what the book is yet', that enabled me to dig deeper and work harder (her compliments and love for Evelyn meant the world too). All the Hachettians enveloped me too. Without them, this book wouldn't be an actual book. Thanks again to editors Deonie Fiford and Rebecca Allen for the final polish, proofreader Rebecca Hamilton (plot hole finder extraordinaire), the boss ladies Louise Stark and Fiona Hazard, and the publicity, marketing and sales teams – I know how hard you work.

Actual lastly, Mr Green's passion for model trains and handmade hay bales was invaluable, as was the man on the tram who sipped his water so elegantly – without him, there'd be no Phillip. Cheers, also, to Policeman Brendan's rundown on L18s over a beer. The laundromat etiquette debates with randoms in caravan parks and my local paint store man sure helped too. So did Lego.

I hear of disciplined writers who diligently ply their trade on the daily. I am not one of those writers. When Sully looks in on me and sees me playing Lego, he tells the other housemates that I'm busy writing . . . because I am.

Hilde Hinton avoided being a writer for many years. But after her critically acclaimed debut novel, *The Loudness of Unsaid Things*, made a number of bestseller lists, everything changed. Now the stories won't stop. Hilde, dedicated big sister to Connie and Samuel Johnson, lives in a boisterous house in Melbourne with a revolving door for the temporarily defeated and takes great pride in people leaving slightly better than when they arrived. Her children are mostly loved. And so are her books.

hachette
AUSTRALIA

If you would like to find out more about Hachette Australia,
our authors, upcoming events and new releases, you can visit
our website or our social media channels:

hachette.com.au

 HachetteAustralia

HachetteAus